"You are special, Jane,"

her mother said softly. "God made you just the way you are, and I am glad."

Jane turned to meet her mother's stare, angered that her mother would say such a thing, yet having too much respect to blurt out her bitter feelings.

Her mother read her face. "You are not ugly or gawky, and you mustn't compare yourself to others." Her mother touched Jane's chin and turned her head toward her once again. "There is nothing wrong with the way you are. You are beautiful in your own way, and one day some man is going to see you for the way you are: beautiful inside and out."

DENISE HUNTER lives in Indiana with her husband and three active, young sons. As the only female of the household, every day is a new adventure, but Denise holds on to the belief that her most important responsibility in this life is to raise her children in such a way that they will love and fear the Lord. *Stranger's Bride* was her first published novel. The message Denise wants her writing to convey is that "God needs to be the center of our lives. If He isn't, everything else is out of kilter."

Books by Denise Hunter

HEARTSONG PRESENTS
HP328—Stranger's Bride

Never a Bride

Denise Hunter

Heartsong Presents

Dedicated with love to my parents:
Sheri and Bill Huston, and Gary and Marsha Waters.

A note from the author:
*I love to hear from my readers! You may correspond with me
by writing:*   **Denise Hunter**
                      Author Relations
                      PO Box 719
                      Uhrichsville, OH 44683

ISBN 1-57748-936-5

NEVER A BRIDE

Cover illustration by Randy Hamblin.

PRINTED IN THE U.S.A.

one

Jane and Cassy Cooper wove their way through the skeletal frame of their family's unfinished restaurant. Jane watched as her sister stepped onto a discarded piece of lumber and strolled the length of it with balance and poise.

"Be sure you're back by nightfall, girls!" Mama called from the soon-to-be kitchen.

"We will." Jane slipped through the framed wall and stepped down to join Cassy on the ground.

Their skirts swished in unison as they headed through the town of Cedar Springs, the warm spring air brushing past Jane's slicked-back hair and cooling her neck. Jane stepped around a deep groove in the rutted street; Cassy hopped over it.

"David told me to follow the path behind the church. I should've brought my cane pole," Cassy said.

"You know Mama doesn't approve of your fishing. You should spend your time in more ladylike pursuits—like sewing. Why, you could open your own shop if you wished."

"I do enjoy making dresses." Cassy's eyes lit with enthusiasm. "How about if I make one for you, Jane? I saw a bolt of periwinkle blue in Parnell's just the other day. The color would really suit you."

Jane snapped her gaze away from Cassy's face. "I own plenty of dresses. Make one for yourself or Katy. She adores getting new clothes."

"Katy and I have dozens of gowns. Besides, all your gowns are brown, or gray, or beige." Jane could tell that Cassy was wrinkling her nose just by the sound of her voice.

Jane sniffed indignantly. "And what's wrong with those colors anyway?"

"They're so plain!"

Jane lowered her gaze and watched her simple gray skirt flutter next to Cassy's ruffled one. The contrast between the two gowns exemplified the differences between the sisters.

Cassy's voice gentled. "Oh, Jane. You could look truly lovely if you only gave it a little effort."

"I'm satisfied with the way I am." . . *And, when will you realize—I'm not like the rest of the family?* Jane added in silent retort as a wagon, clattering in the distance, diverted her sister's attentions.

"Look. Here comes my Caleb!" Cassy clutched Jane's sleeve.

Jane focused on the nearing wagon and sighed with dismay. "And, Luke."

Luke pulled the reins, and the horses halted in front of them.

"Hello, Cassy. Jane." Caleb nodded in greeting to both girls, but scarcely took his eyes off his fiancée.

Cassy stepped closer to the wagon, and Jane followed reluctantly.

"What brings you to town?" Cassy asked.

"We just had to pick up some—"

Suddenly, Jane's boot caught in a rut, and she went sprawling forward. Her hands, groping desperately for a handhold, collided with warm horseflesh instead. The smelly beast raised his nose and whinnied in protest.

Jane struggled to regain her balance as the sound of rude laughter reached her ears. She narrowed her eyes at Luke Reiley. Why couldn't he just leave her alone?

"Are you all right, Jane?" Cassy asked.

"Perfectly," she insisted, brushing an imaginary speck from her bodice.

"The ruts are bad right now due to all that rain last week," Caleb said, exuding charm. "How've you been, Miss Jane?"

"Just fine, thank you." She tossed Caleb a weak smile before shooting a glare toward his obnoxious brother.

Luke tipped his hat, his brown eyes flickering with mischief. "Jane. Cassy. Can we give you a lift somewhere?"

"No!"

"Yes, please."

The sisters responded simultaneously. Cassy giggled. Jane shifted awkwardly.

"Well now," Luke said. "Does that mean we take you halfway there and let you off, or does that mean we take one of you and leave the other?"

Everyone laughed except for Jane, who felt heat climbing to the tips of her ears. She needn't question which of the two sisters he'd prefer to leave behind!

"Actually, we're on our way to the spring," Cassy said, "so you couldn't take us very far, anyway."

"We'd best be on our way, Cassy, if we're going to make it back by dark." Although her words were true, Jane's real reason for wanting to go had nothing to do with impending nightfall and everything to do with one irritating man.

The group said good-bye and, as Luke snapped the reins, Jane released her breath.

"See you two tomorrow night," Caleb called, referring

to the engagement party that Cassy's parents had planned.

The sisters stood by the roadside and watched the wagon clamor away. "Isn't he divine, Jane? I can't believe God made such a wonderful man!" Cassy spun in a circle of delight.

"You are, undoubtedly, referring to Caleb. For, heaven knows, his brother is God's curse upon me! Utterly childish!" she mumbled.

Cassy laughed merrily and tapped Jane on the arm. "Jane! What a perfectly awful thing to say about your future brother-in-law!"

"Don't remind me!"

"And he can't be as childish as you think; he did hold things together when their parents died. Caleb has nothing but praise for him. He only teases you so because of the way you react."

"Like I said, childish!"

≈

Luke stepped through the door and shucked his worn, brown boots.

"Is that you, Caleb?" Esther, their housekeeper, called from the kitchen.

"No, Luke. Caleb's tending the team. Is there something I can help you with?" Luke asked as he padded into the kitchen.

"Yes, could you holler at Elizabeth and tell her supper's ready?" Esther placed the platter of fried chicken on the table with the other food. Then, she filled plates for herself and her husband, covering them with cheesecloth.

Luke held the door for her as she left. "I'll see you in the morning, Esther."

"Have a good evening, Luke."

Just as Esther exited the front door, Elizabeth burst through the back door. "Hi, Luke! Ummm. Fried chicken, my favorite!"

"Wash your hands. I waited for you."

Elizabeth pumped water into the basin and splashed around for a moment. "Where's Caleb? Are we eating without him?"

"He'll be in shortly. He said to save him a plate."

Elizabeth and Luke took their seats at the table. Although their ma and pa had been gone for nearly three years, the Reiley children still sat in the same seats they always had. Luke may have taken his father's place as the head of the family, but his place at the head of the table remained empty.

When Caleb came in, he seated himself while Elizabeth filled a plate with food. Caleb wore a boyish grin, and Luke could tell he was in especially good spirits. And why shouldn't he be? He was engaged to Cassy—the woman of his dreams.

And, the woman of Luke's dreams.

Luke finished eating, then settled in his fireside chair while Caleb pretended to peruse a menu.

"Let's see here," he said with a pompous voice. "Yes, miss. I do believe I'll have the fried chicken. And perhaps a bit of potatoes and a yeast roll."

Elizabeth snickered and tried to maintain a straight face as she set his plate before him. "Here you are, sir."

Elizabeth's brown braids swung as she spun back to the kitchen. She was growing up. Still playing silly games with Caleb, yet soon she would begin to show an interest in boys. Luke nearly groaned. He knew nothing about raising a young woman. *Thank the Lord for Esther,* he thought.

"I'm all finished in the kitchen, Luke. I'm going outside to play."

"Be sure you are back by dark."

She rolled her eyes. "You say that every night." She opened the door and stepped over the threshold.

Luke opened his mouth, but before he could speak, Elizabeth said, "I know. . . . Be sure and shut the door." She tossed Luke an impertinent grin and vaulted down the steps.

"She sure has you pegged!" Caleb said.

"Well, somebody has to play the nag around here."

"And a fine job you do, sir."

"Thank you."

Caleb took a swig of lemonade. "The Coopers' restaurant and inn are sure going up fast. They're hoping to open the restaurant in July and the hotel a month or so later." Caleb paused, then shook his head slowly. "I still can't believe Cassy's going to marry me! Sometimes it's like a dream. Isn't she just the sweetest thing?"

Luke swallowed hard. "We've never exactly had the same taste in women."

"That's true enough!" Caleb laid his fork down with a clank. "Are you sure you don't mind if Cassy and I take your room? My room would do just fine."

Luke's stomach tightened in a painful knot, but he forced his face to form a grin. "It's only right. Newlyweds need their privacy." The words stuck like glue in his throat. Was Caleb convinced? He looked over at his brother. Caleb wore a dazed grin and seemed oblivious to everything but his own thoughts.

Caleb hardly noticed when Luke said good night and retired to his bedroom, just off the main room. After closing the door, he sank down on the large bed against the wall. The pale light of dusk filtered through the beige curtains his mother had sewn years ago. How he missed his parents. In times such as this, he wished his ma were there to advise him. What would she tell him to do?

I guess you'd better get on your knees, Luke. The answer came quickly, as though she had answered herself.

Luke rolled off the bed and assumed his favorite praying position. Years ago, his ma told him that the best way to humble yourself before God was to get on your knees. He had seen her in that position more times than he could count.

At first, Luke simply closed his eyes and attempted to order his thoughts. Then, he prayed silently. *Dear heavenly Father, I'm confused about my feelings for Cassy. You know I want Your perfect will for my life and for my family. You know what my thoughts were when I met Cassy. I felt so certain that she was right for me, and I was so excited about finding someone special. I don't know why You allowed me to fall for Cassy before I knew she and Caleb had feelings for one another. But I thank You that no one knows of my feelings so they don't have to feel guilty or feel bad for me. Thank You for bringing Caleb happiness.*

Please remove these feelings from me, Lord. Help me as we all try to live together in the same house. Give me a clean, pure heart, Father. In Jesus' name, amen.

two

The day of the party dawned clear blue and a bit windy. Anna, Cassy, Jane, and Katy worked diligently to prepare the feast while Eli and David set up tables and chairs in the backyard.

The day held an air of festivity and excitement, amplified by Eli and Anna, who had been dropping hints of a surprise for Caleb and Cassy. None of the children knew the secret and, as much as they tried, they were unable to extract the information from their parents.

Caleb, Luke, and Elizabeth arrived on schedule, and Cassy was released from her duties to entertain their guests. When supper was ready, Jane and her mother carried the food outside, and the two families gathered around the table to say grace.

Somehow Luke ended up beside Jane. Since, on her other side, Cassy and Caleb were thoroughly absorbed in one another, Jane focused on her food. Luke, however, seemed determined to pester her.

"So, Jane, have you been busy helping Cassy with wedding plans?" Luke asked just as she took a mouthful of ham.

She hurried to swallow and choked, initiating a fit of coughing that surely turned her face an uncomely shade of red. She grabbed her glass of lemonade, gave one last unladylike hack, then drained the cup dry.

Jane looked around and was relieved that the noisy party carried on, oblivious to her episode.

Luke, however, sat staring at her with concerned amusement, one eyebrow hiked high on his forehead.

Irritated, Jane set her glass back on the table only to realize that the glass she had drained was not hers, but Luke's. She breathed a sigh and hissed, "Looks like I drank your lemonade."

Luke threw his head back and guffawed, holding his stomach as if he could not contain himself. Jane stiffened and opened her mouth to offer a rebuttal, when a clinking noise drew her attention to the head of the table where her father stood.

"May I have your attention, please?" When the clamor subsided, her father continued. "Thank you. Cassy, Caleb, we are here in your honor to celebrate the union of our families. Anna and I couldn't be happier with Cassy's choice for a husband." Eli paused as murmurs of agreement followed. "Cassy, as you may have guessed, your mother and I have a surprise for you and your soon-to-be husband." He paused as if to let the anticipation build. "We have arranged a four-week trip to California for your honeymoon!"

Cassy gasped and looked to her future husband.

Caleb sat with his mouth agape. "That's very generous, Mr. Cooper," Caleb said. "But, the ranch—"

Eli interrupted. "I knew the ranch would be your first concern, son. That's why I cleared this with Luke first." He nodded and winked at Luke. "We have an agreement. If he needs any help while you're away, David will step in." David smiled and nodded to Caleb. "And, of course, Esther will still be here to look after Elizabeth and the house. Everything's been arranged!"

"Oh, Papa. Mama. I don't know what to say!"

"That would be a first!" David said. The group erupted in laughter.

"What a wonderful surprise, Mr. and Mrs. Cooper. Cassy and I thank you from the bottom of our hearts."

Everyone resumed their meals, and Jane listened to Cassy chatter about what she would wear and what they would see.

All the while, Jane's heart ached. She knew she would never have all this—a wedding, a honeymoon, a husband—things that came easily to girls like Cassy and Katy. No matter what her mother said, it's what's on the outside that counts. Now it was Cassy's turn, and in a few years it would be Katy's. As sure as the moon hung in the sky, Jane knew that her turn would never come.

And, yet, some tiny piece of her heart clung desperately to the hope that she might be wrong.

❧

May brought more wind and rain. Construction on the building slowed due to the inclement weather, and the postponement gave the Cooper family time to plan for the June wedding. Cassy's head had been in the clouds in the recent weeks, and her family frequently teased her about her absentmindedness.

Anna Cooper lamented over the absence of her own wedding gown, which they had been forced to leave behind when they moved from Philadelphia. Cassy, too elated over her upcoming marriage to be depressed about anything, enlisted Jane to sketch a gown and, together, they designed the wedding dress. Cassy immediately went to work sewing the gown. The Reverend Hill was asked to officiate the wedding, and Mrs. Leighton, who ran the post office, insisted Cassy take whatever flowers she needed from her plentiful garden.

Soon, the month of May slipped by, and the wedding was just days away. Every moment seemed filled with sewing, planning, and writing letters to friends back home. These tasks were somehow squeezed into the normal duties of meals, laundry, and cleaning. A regular schedule of construction had resumed once the wet spring days had given way to a warm, sunny June.

The Reileys had been invited to dinner on more than one occasion. Jane kept herself busy with Elizabeth when they were there, making sure that she was not seated beside Luke again. He still managed to annoy her and seemed to derive great pleasure from harassing her.

Now, two days before the big event, there was a lull in the activity. Everything was ready except for the flowers.

Jane seized the opportunity of the hiatus to escape to the backyard and draw. She found a magnificent view of the hills there, and she had been wanting to capture the scene on paper since their move to Cedar Springs. Her easel was still packed away, so Jane propped herself against a tree, a pad of paper resting on her bent legs.

Jane heard approaching footsteps as she attempted to duplicate the shadow of the hill's crevice. "Good morning, Cassy," she said without ceasing her work. Since Jane sat, somewhat hidden, on the ground amid the flora, Cassy startled at the greeting and halted her steps.

"Oh. Jane. It's you."

Cassy's forlorn voice drew Jane's attention, and she laid down her tools. "You sound troubled, Cassy. Did something happen?"

Cassy walked over to Jane and dropped down beside her. "Caleb just came by with some bad news."

"What? Not the wedding. . . ."

"No! No, nothing like that." The corners of Cassy's lips drew up in a simulated smile. "But, Esther's daughter in Springfield suffered some kind of accident. Evidently, the damage is permanent, and she needs help with her children. Esther and her husband are moving back home to help out. They're leaving in five days."

"So Esther won't be able to care for Elizabeth and the household."

"Right. I'll take over her tasks, and Caleb figures we can live in the cottage they stayed in. That'll be nice, I suppose." Cassy sighed. "Still, we won't be able to take our trip to California. I feel just awful sniveling over that when Esther's daughter has suffered a real tragedy, but I was so looking forward to the honeymoon. I've always wanted to go to California, and we had the trip all planned." Cassy's lips tipped up at the corners. "Well, there's nothing to be done about it."

Suddenly Cassy straightened, and her head snapped toward Jane. "Oh!"

"What? What is it?"

Cassy slumped. "No. Never mind. It's nothing."

"Well, it must be something!"

"Really, Jane. It's too much to ask."

"*What* is too much to ask?

"I was just going to say, maybe you could fill in for

Esther while Caleb and I are away." Cassy watched as Jane shrank away in dread. "Like I said. It's too much to ask."

"Cassy, I. . ."

"It's all right." She laid her hand on Jane's. "Really. I know you don't care much for Luke." Cassy made another effort at a smile. "I just need to count my blessings. In two days I'm going to marry the man I love, and he's more wonderful than I ever imagined." Cassy pulled herself up. "Thanks for listening, Jane. I do feel better. I'd better go and put those finishing touches on my gown."

Jane watched her go, a sick feeling churning in her stomach that could not be attributed to food or illness. She felt horribly selfish. She could solve Cassy and Caleb's problem; she could make their wedding all they wanted it to be.

But she didn't want to because of Luke.

Perhaps Katy. . . Just as quickly, she dismissed the idea. Katy was hopeless in the kitchen. She had always been relegated to table setting and dish washing since she had single-handedly burnt an entire supper. She would love to see the look on Luke's face when presented with supper Katy-style! The thought of arranging such an event proved tempting. Still, when she thought of Elizabeth, she knew she couldn't carry out such a devious plan.

Jane picked up her sketch pad and continued her work. She wished she could will away her guilty conscience. Cassy had been so happy in recent weeks. What a shame that these latest developments now cast a shadow over the wedding!

Maybe her taking Esther's place wouldn't be so bad. After all, Luke would be gone all day, leaving her and Elizabeth alone. She would only have to endure him at breakfast and supper. Perhaps she could even leave after preparing supper. Then, she would hardly see him at all.

Jane put away her supplies. She was doing more thinking than drawing, anyway. As she followed the stone path toward the house, she decided she would accept this dreadful assignment—for Cassy. It was a small thing, really, and she knew Cassy would do the same for her.

Within the next few hours, everything was arranged. Cassy and Luke would go to California, and Jane would stay in Esther's cottage until the honeymooners returned.

three

Jane spent the next day making floral arrangements for the church and a bouquet for Cassy. Because of her creative ability, she was given free rein on this task. Cassy and Anna prepared several appetizing dishes for the small reception, which was to be held at the Coopers' house. Then, they turned their attentions to decorating the wedding cake.

Finally, the wedding day arrived, and the house bustled with activity. An early morning rain shower gave them a bit of a fright, but soon the clouds rolled by and left a clear blue expanse in their place.

They arrived at the church on time, despite several last-minute catastrophes: a missing button, lost shoes, and a search for "something borrowed." The ceremony was brief, but beautiful. Jane noticed her mother wiping away a tear or two, and Jane herself swallowed around a lump in her throat.

After the wedding, the families moved to the Coopers' house, where they ate wedding cake and celebrated. Soon, the time approached for the newlyweds to leave for Wichita in order to catch their train.

As Caleb and Cassy dashed down the porch steps, Jane tossed a handful of white rice into the air and watched as it showered down upon them. The couple ducked under the barrage of grain, their laughter an echo of the fanfare that surrounded them.

Cassy's cheeks matched the rosy traveling dress she had laboriously stitched. Her honey-blond hair was in casual disarray around her radiant face, but Jane couldn't help but wonder if any other woman could look so beautiful with flecks of rice clinging to her hair.

When the couple drew to a halt at the base of the steps, Cassy threw a glance over her shoulder before hurling her fresh bouquet directly at her older sister.

Jane put out her hands to fend off the impending object but, a moment later, found herself holding the cluster she had arranged only the day before. Pursing her lips, she sent Cassy a scowl and received in return a giggle and a wink.

As the newlyweds walked toward the wagon, the Reiley and Cooper families swarmed them. Eli and Anna walked nearest their daughter, followed closely by Luke and Elizabeth.

Jane followed at a distance, content to watch the good-byes from the outskirts. A hot gust of wind caught the skirt of her new beige gown, and it swirled rebelliously around her legs.

"Don't let Caleb get too used to lazing around, Cassy!" Luke called to his new sister-in-law. "Four weeks away, and he'll probably come back completely useless!"

"I can keep up with you any day, big brother!" Caleb flicked the brim of Luke's hat, causing it to tip back, and everyone laughed. Jane watched as the hat's shadow receded from Luke's face.

As she studied his eyes and his smile, she noticed something odd about his expression. Not anything definably different. But, something. . . Just then he turned away, and

Jane decided her imagination must be working overtime. And, why should the matter concern her, anyway? She didn't care one whit about Luke Reiley!

Jane stepped forward for her good-bye hug, then slipped to the outside of the group. Luke's turn came next, and Jane watched from behind her sister as he embraced her, his sinewy arms sliding around Cassy's narrow waist. Because of her position, only Jane fell privy to the look on Luke's face.

Nothing she had learned about Luke during their three-month acquaintance had prepared her for what she saw in that moment. His twinkling eyes turned dull and lifeless. A frown pulled his lips downward, swallowing his one dimple. Luke's eyelids fell like the lid of a coffin, and his Adam's apple bobbed once as if swallowing a mass of emotion.

His obvious struggle for control melted Jane's frozen heart for an instant.

Luke's jaw hardened. Then, he released Cassy. "You honeymooners better be off or you're going to miss your train!" His smile made Jane wonder, once again, if she'd been seeing things.

Caleb helped Cassy into the wagon. She settled her full skirt around her, then laughed as Caleb swept his felt hat off his head and took a royal bow before their families. Once seated, Caleb snapped the reins, setting the two bays in motion. The families waved, their faces alight with joy as they watched the newlyweds pull out. Laughter and shouts of good-bye, delivered with enthusiasm, were snatched away by the June wind.

Jane had watched the day's events with mixed feelings.

She was happy for Cassy, but the day also signified a big change in Jane's life. Her sister would no longer be right there when Jane needed to talk. No one else understood her the way Cassy did.

Jane also longed for a special someone, and she was irritated with herself for even thinking of such things. Until recent weeks, she thought the issue was settled in her mind. She had made up her mind on the school playground long ago. She would never have a husband.

Now, as Jane watched Cassy and Caleb ride off to Wichita, her thoughts turned in an entirely different direction. Luke loved Cassy. This man, who had vexed her for the past three months, was in love with her sister. She was certain. No other explanation could account for the pain she had seen in his face. The realization of this truth shook Jane to the bone. Oh, she didn't wonder that he could love Cassy—for who could help but adore her? But, how could he have kept his affections hidden all this time?

Did anyone else know? Surely not Caleb nor Cassy, for if Cassy had known, she would have confided in Jane. And she would have felt just awful!

For the first time, Jane felt something other than irritation for Luke. Her current feelings bordered on compassion—quickly heading toward pity.

That is, until Luke whispered into her ear, scaring two years off her life.

"You're gonna crush your pretty flowers."

Jane realized that she had been twisting a daisy rather viciously. Several petals lay on the ground at her feet. "They're not my flowers," she snapped.

"Of course they are. You caught them."

"I didn't catch them! Cassy threw them at me!"

"Well, they did land in your hands." Luke's eyes crinkled at the corners. He spoke again before she could retort. "It's sure gonna be an interesting four weeks!" He sauntered off, shaking his head, and leaving Jane exasperated once again.

four

The next morning, Jane forced her weary body out of bed. Throughout the night of elusive sleep, yesterday's wedding replayed in her mind. She could not erase from her memory the pain sheathed in Luke's face the previous day. Had she misinterpreted his expression? Mistaken some other emotion for despair?

She didn't think so. An observer by nature, Jane tended to circle the edge of the action, a convenient spot for deciphering peoples' motives and feelings. The habit helped her sketch realistic portraits and, if she had sketched Luke's face yesterday, she was sure she could have captured the anguish she had seen.

Jane descended the stairs in her gray dress and joined her mother and Katy in the kitchen. Breakfast was accomplished with little fuss since everyone was drained from the workload of the previous weeks. In short order, the family was in the carriage and on their way to church.

Katy joined her new friends in the churchyard, and David went off to speak with one of the men who had been helping with the construction. Jane entered the building with her mother and father, and they took their seats in an empty pew.

Soon church started, and Luke went forward to lead the music. Jane kept her eyes on the new hymnals, knowing Luke would embarrass her if given the chance.

After the song, the Reverend Hill stepped forward, and Jane took this as her cue to let her mind wander. She relived the wedding and wondered where Cassy and Caleb were now. Then, her thoughts drifted on to other subjects in an effort to pass the time. She mentally planned the noon meal. Chose the subject for her next painting. Packed her bags for her stay at the Reileys'.

At the end of the closing prayer, Jane heaved a sigh and looked sideways to see her mother watching her. "What is it, Mama?" she asked.

Her mother gave a sad half-smile. "Nothing, sweetie."

Later that day, Jane packed her bags in record time since she had already planned what to take. Tomorrow she would move into the cottage. She wished the four weeks were already behind her.

&

The next day, after breakfast was cleared, Jane stepped out to the porch and sank onto the wooden swing. A low fog smothered the town with an oppressive presence and, off in the distance, the hills that projected from the blanket of white seemed to be floating in midair. The air was thick with the smell of rain, and Jane pondered how perfectly the weather reflected her mood.

Her short reprieve ended when her mother called her name, and the day passed quickly as she moved from one chore to the next. Soon it was evening and, after supper, her father took her to the Reileys'.

As they drove along the dirt drive that led to the Reiley house and cottage, Jane studied Luke's ranch. Prairie grass covered the ground almost as far as the eye could see. Trees and cattle sprinkled the landscape, as if to break up the monotony, and the ever-present ridge of distant hills provided a calming sense of security.

The trees and shrubbery drew closer together as they drove along and, when they approached a grove of oak trees, Jane saw why the previous owners had built on this spot. Foliage obscured the main house but, when they neared, they saw the cottage in a clearing to the left and the barns off to the right.

The clattering wagon must have alerted Luke and Elizabeth to their approach, for as her father halted in front of the cottage, they emerged from the house.

Luke offered his hand to Jane to help her from the wagon. Since her father was already alighting from the other side, she saw no polite way to decline Luke's assistance. She put her hand in his and stepped down. She turned to retrieve her bag, but Luke was quicker. "I've got it," he said, then rounded the wagon and shook Eli's hand. "Evening, sir. Thank you for bringing Jane."

"Good evening, Luke, Elizabeth. I was glad to bring her. First rest I've had all day."

Elizabeth addressed Jane. "I'm so happy you've come, Jane! Come, and I'll show you the cottage." Luke stayed by the wagon talking to her father while Jane and Elizabeth followed the stone path to the cottage. "I cleaned the place up today and put fresh linens on the bed. The cottage is small but homey. I hope you like it."

Elizabeth pushed open the squeaky wooden door, and Jane followed her inside. To the left was the sitting room filled with a potpourri of serviceable furniture. Against the left wall, a stack of dry logs framed a small fireplace and an oval carpet hugged the plank floor in front of the hearth.

A sawbuck table, surrounded by four Windsor chairs, dominated the eating room to her right. Straight ahead was the door that led, presumably, to the bedroom. To the right of that loomed the kitchen.

Elizabeth interrupted her appraisal. "I hope everything is okay. I know you're not used to small quarters." She seemed worried that Jane would be displeased, so Jane reassured her.

"Nonsense! After all, there's only me, and I don't take up much space. Besides, I think you're right. It is homey." Jane wandered into the bedroom, which contained a bed, bureau, table, and chest of drawers. Atop the mahogany bureau, a vase of fresh cut flowers commanded center stage. She walked over to them and inhaled their sweet fragrance. "Ummm. These are beautiful; how thoughtful of you."

"Oh, I didn't pick them. Luke did." Elizabeth spun around and headed toward the kitchen. "The kitchen's in here, but I guess you'll be doing all your cooking at our house. I can help you. I'm a good cook."

"I'm sure you are." Jane followed, her mind still on the flowers.

"The bathtub is under this cabinet. There's a pump in the backyard, or we have one in our kitchen if you want to use that."

Just then Luke entered the house, followed by her father. Luke gently dropped Jane's bag to the floor. "I appreciate your help, Jane. I couldn't have managed with both Caleb and Esther gone."

Jane avoided Luke's eyes, uncomfortable with his gratitude. "Don't be silly. I could hardly have let Cassy and

Caleb miss their trip."

Jane's father surveyed the room. "Well, your mama's gonna miss your help, that's for sure." He turned to Luke. "Anna's always telling me, 'Jane's my right hand.' But, speaking of Anna, I'd best be getting back to her. Jane, if you need anything, just get word to me."

"I'll be fine, Papa."

Luke shook her father's hand again. "I'll make sure of it, sir. She's practically family, after all." He winked at Jane, seeming to enjoy her discomfort.

Luke and Elizabeth left, too, and Jane was grateful for the chance to unpack and settle in. She was unaccustomed to the quiet that now permeated the little house, but the solitude was a pleasant change.

After tucking away her clothes in the drawers, she changed into her white nightgown and lay down on the mattress, which, she was dismayed to find, was filled with straw rather than feathers. She blew out the candle on the bedside table, lay back on the pillow and, quicker than she could have imagined, sleep's oblivion claimed her.

&

When she opened her eyes the next morning, it took a moment for Jane to remember where she was. Dawn's early light seeped into the room, and she knew the sun would be up soon. She stretched, then sat up in the bed that crackled beneath her.

After donning a brown muslin dress, she walked the short distance to the main house. When she approached the door, she stood frozen in indecision. Should she knock or just go right in? Deciding on the former, she had just raised her hand to knock when the door flew open.

"Good morning, Jane!" Elizabeth said. "I'm headed out to milk the cows. The kitchen is right there," she said as she pointed to the left. "If you can't find anything, just holler and I'll come show you where it is."

"Good enough. Is Luke awake?"

"Oh, yes. He's in the stable, I imagine. We usually eat about six o'clock, but whenever you have the food ready, we can eat. I'll be back in a little bit to help."

"Fine, Elizabeth."

Jane set to work in the kitchen, which wasn't fancy, but much nicer than the cottage's. The cooking utensils were efficiently located, and she could tell Esther had been a very organized woman. After surveying the pantry, Jane decided on buckwheat cakes, eggs, and sausages. The coffee was already made, so she began mixing the buckwheat batter.

Breakfast was well underway by the time Elizabeth joined her. The younger girl set the table and poured milk, all the while twittering like a spring bird. As breakfast neared completion, Jane began to wonder whether Luke would be joining them. She found herself glancing at the door periodically and knew her nerves were strung from the waiting and wondering. If only she were not so awkward! Luke's very nature seemed to magnify that awkwardness, and it was this that she dreaded. Elizabeth's presence would help, but still, she wished she had not gotten herself into this.

৯

Luke's mind spun as he did his morning chores. He wondered where Caleb and Cassy were and what they were doing. His mind had been filled these last few days with torturous thoughts. Saturday night he had come home from the wedding and worked. He had cleaned every gun in the house, mucked out the stalls and filled them with fresh hay, and fixed a wagon wheel; anything to occupy his mind. Elizabeth must have thought him mad, but she was too young to understand the situation.

One good thing about this all-fired predicament—no one knew how he felt. He'd done a fine job at putting on an act. Why, he could be a player in one of those traveling theater shows he'd once seen. Yep, he'd fooled them all.

He flung the pitchfork to the ground in a rare display of temper. No one knew his dilemma, and that meant he had no one in whom he could confide. No friend's advice would be forthcoming about what he should do when his brother and sister-in-law returned from their honeymoon. No advice about how he was supposed to see Cassy at every meal, every day for the rest of his life, and keep from wanting her. No advice on how to live with the fact that he loved his brother's wife.

How immoral could he get? Loving the woman his brother had just married.

Luke dropped onto a bale of hay and covered his face with shaking hands. *What am I gonna do, God? You've got to get me out of this. How am I supposed to live here, so close to the woman I love, and keep my thoughts pure? I feel like I've betrayed Caleb in the worst way, and he doesn't even know it. Help me, Lord.*

Luke sat there for some time neglecting his chores. Finally, his rumbling stomach convinced him it was time for breakfast. He stopped by the pump on his way and splashed cold water on his face before going in to face Elizabeth and Jane.

⁊

Jane had just placed the platter of sausages on the table when she heard the front door open, then slam shut. Luke rounded the corner a moment later. "Sorry, didn't mean to slam the door." He gave a crooked, almost contrite, grin. "Good morning, Jane."

"Morning. Breakfast is ready."

Elizabeth and Luke took their seats while Jane finished setting the food on the table. She surveyed the situation as she worked. Luke and Elizabeth sat across from each other, so she could sit at either end of the table, beside Elizabeth or beside Luke. Elizabeth made the decision easy.

"You can sit by me, Jane. That's where Caleb usually sits."

Jane took her seat and, after they joined hands, Luke offered the grace. Elizabeth did most of the talking throughout the meal, and Luke was unusually quiet. Jane wondered if Cassy was on his mind. She'd never seen him so withdrawn.

Luke finished his meal before Jane and Elizabeth, then excused himself. "The food was great, Jane. I'll be out in the northern pastures today, so I won't be back for lunch." Luke crammed his black hat onto his head. "I'll just grab some apples and bread from the kitchen."

Luke disappeared into the kitchen and returned a few minutes later with a bulging leather bag. "See you at supper. I usually get back around six o'clock."

"I wonder what's on his mind?" Elizabeth said after he left. "I don't think I've seen him so quiet since Mama and Papa died."

"I was wondering about that myself."

"Maybe it has something to do with Caleb getting married."

Jane feared that Elizabeth was a little too close to the truth. "He's probably just having a bad morning."

Elizabeth giggled. "Luke? He doesn't have bad mornings. That's Caleb! You should see him in the morning. He won't even talk until he's had two cups of coffee, and even after that, you'll only get a grunt!"

"Sounds as if I'm lucky to be leaving when they return."

The day passed quickly, with Elizabeth showing her what needed to be done. Obviously, Esther did all the work a mother would normally do: cooking, cleaning, laundry, sewing, weeding. They were all familiar tasks, and Jane had no trouble taking over once Elizabeth showed her where things were kept.

While Jane worked, Elizabeth played nearby or helped with the task. Weeding was the chore that seemed most neglected, so Jane started on that immediately after breakfast. Later in the day, she cleaned the floors upstairs and down until they gleamed.

Elizabeth tried to persuade her to go for a ride, but Jane made it clear—riding horses was something she did not do! Ever since she'd seen little Billy Earnheart fall to his death all those years ago, she'd been terrified of the creatures. After Elizabeth insisted that Luke wouldn't mind, Jane finally agreed to let the young girl take a ride alone.

By the time supper rolled around, Jane was ready for a rest but knew she had to get supper on the table. A visit to the root cellar turned up pork and potatoes, which she prepared with Elizabeth's help. There was enough bread for the next couple days, but she knew she would have to make more soon.

As she worked, she planned how she would fill a plate and excuse herself so that she could eat alone. She didn't mind Elizabeth's company. Luke, however, was an aggravation to be avoided, and if she managed to escape supper tonight, she would set the standard for the following days.

While Jane placed the food on the table, Luke came in and washed up at the kitchen basin. When he and Elizabeth seated themselves, Jane took her filled plate from on top of the stove and turned to address the brother and sister. "Have a nice supper. I'll be in the cottage if you need me."

Elizabeth turned to look at Jane and, across from Elizabeth, Luke froze. An awkward moment of silence ensued before Luke spoke. "Why, you can eat right here with us, Jane. I wouldn't dream of sending you off to eat all by yourself." Luke's face wore a crooked grin, and there were little crinkles at the corners of his eyes.

"Oh, it's no bother," Jane said. "Elizabeth told me Esther took her supper home to eat, so I thought I'd do the same."

Luke laughed. "Yes, well, Esther had a husband at home to feed. Now unless you're secretly married and hiding a husband in that cottage, you may as well just take a seat with us."

Jane pursed her lips and moved to take a seat. Vexing man! Now she had to stay. Luke said the prayer, but Jane heard none of it. No one had ever irritated her as much as this man. Why, he'd even had the gall to poke fun at her for being unmarried. Not everyone was appealing to the eye and able to attract the opposite sex. But what would he know about that? He with his shiny brown hair and dimpled grin. He may be single still, but his unmarried state was obviously his choice.

When the prayer ended, Jane stabbed at her pork and proceeded to absentmindedly pick at the meal she had prepared. Conversation flowed between Luke and Elizabeth, but Jane's responses were limited to single words and short phrases. As soon as she could graciously do so, she excused herself from the table and began the cleanup process. Elizabeth joined her a moment later and, when the kitchen was put back in order, Jane said good night and escaped to the cottage.

five

Thursday and Friday passed with relative ease. Jane did familiar chores and got into a comfortable routine. On Saturday morning she made bread, then sewed a tear in one of Elizabeth's dresses while the bread was rising. After kneading the dough, she changed the bedding.

Elizabeth had gone out to play, and Jane was carrying the bedding down the stairs when she heard a wagon pull into the yard. Curious to see who the visitor was, Jane dropped the bedding by the foot of the stairs and went to the door. She didn't need a looking glass to know she was in no condition for company. Her hair, which was tied in a knot at her neck, had come loose and hung in strings around her face. She was wearing her frumpiest gray gown, which had no adornment whatsoever, and a dingy apron, dusted with flour.

Jane opened the door to see a very pregnant woman awkwardly alighting from a buckboard with the help of an older woman. She recognized the first woman as Sara McClain, whom she had spoken with a time or two at church. The other woman, Hetty, helped on the ranch.

Even her advanced pregnancy could not conceal Sara's beauty. Her hair on this hot, June day was worn up, but the curly ends of her hair hung from the top of her head, creating a halo effect. Her appearance made Jane feel dowdy. Jane stepped onto the porch as the two women approached and pinned a polite smile to her face.

Sara smiled in return. "Good afternoon, Jane," she said as she mounted the porch steps. "You remember Hetty, don't you?"

Jane extended a hand. "Yes, I do. Good afternoon."

Hetty's warm smile extended to her eyes. "How are you getting along here at the Reileys', dear?"

"Just fine, thank you." Jane wished Elizabeth were nearby to fill the silence. "Would you like to come in for a cup of tea or lemonade?"

"Lemonade sounds wonderful." Sara held out the pie she was carrying. "This is for you. I know you probably haven't had time to do much baking."

Jane received the pie graciously, and the women entered the house. Jane showed them into the main room, then returned to the kitchen to pour drinks. When she returned, she saw that Hetty and Sara were admiring the daguerreotype of Mr. and Mrs. Reiley.

"Did you know them?" Jane asked, then reprimanded herself for being so blunt.

Hetty spoke up as if nothing was amiss. "I knew them. We'd been neighbors for about nine years when they died. It was a carriage accident. They were going to Illinois to visit Mrs. Reiley's relations, and there was some mishap with the stagecoach. It rolled down a steep embankment, and all the passengers died. Only the driver lived. It was so sad. These kids only had each other and God. Nathan and Gus, my husband, helped Luke and Caleb with the ranch until they could manage on their own. Caleb had to quit school. Elizabeth was in shock for some time."

"I can only try to imagine how terrible the tragedy was

for them," Jane said.

"I didn't know them at all." Sara scooted back on the sofa until her feet were nearly off the floor. "They had been gone for two years by the time I moved here from Boston."

"What brought you to Cedar Springs?" Jane politely inquired. Hetty and Sara looked at one another and burst into laughter.

Jane was confused by their reaction, but curious to know the reason for it. "What did I say?"

Sara sobered and reassured Jane. "Oh, it was nothing you said, Jane. It's just that I've never been asked that question, and it struck me how incredible my answer will sound."

"She's right," Hetty said. "I don't think I would believe her story if I hadn't been a witness to it."

Jane set her cup on the little table and settled back in her chair. "Please tell me. You've piqued my curiosity."

"Well, like I said, I lived in Boston before. My mother had passed away, and I lived with my stepfather, who was a drunkard. My situation was unpleasant to say the least, and I was searching for a way to escape. I ran across an ad in the *Boston Herald* that advertised for a wife. I responded to the ad, and here I am in Cedar Springs married to the man who placed it, Nathan."

Jane was shocked. "You came all this way to marry a man you had never met? How did you know he was a decent man?" Jane hoped she didn't sound as if she were prying.

"Well, we did exchange letters, and I knew he was a Christian, but I figured my other options were even worse, so I took a chance and came."

"That was very courageous."

"Oh, believe me! I was scared straight. Especially after I saw my groom-to-be."

"She was scared all right," Hetty added. "She was as timid as a lamb in a wolf pack whenever Nathan was around, that is, until they got a better understanding of each other."

Jane recalled the way Nathan stood close to Sara in church, often with an arm draped protectively around her. "Things seem to have worked out well for you."

"I can't tell you how wonderfully. Just over a year ago I was alone and scared, and here I am today married and about to become a mother!" Sara squirmed in her seat.

"When are you due?" Jane asked.

"Last week!" She made a face. "But I don't think junior here has consulted the calendar."

Hetty patted Sara's hand. "Now, child, that baby will come when he's good and ready, and there ain't no doctor can tell him when to be born!"

Sara heaved a sigh. "I know you're right, but if I get any bigger, I think I'm going to burst."

They laughed, and Jane gave her first genuine smile since the ladies came.

"We should be leavin'," Hetty said. "I can tell Sara's back is achin' by the way she won't sit still. Besides, we don't want to wear out our welcome."

"You've done no such thing." Jane rose with the women and escorted them to the door. "It's been refreshing to have company. Sara, I hope that baby comes soon, for your sake. Maybe Elizabeth and I will come by shortly afterwards with some baked goods."

"That would be lovely, Jane." Sara and Hetty mounted the buckboard, and the women waved good-bye.

Jane watched the wagon roll away and realized that, despite her disheveled appearance, she'd felt comfortable around Sara and Hetty; something she couldn't say about many people outside her family.

Elizabeth came running just after the wagon disappeared from sight. "Who was it?" she asked, out of breath from her run.

"Sara and Hetty paid me a call." Jane saw her disappointment and quickly added, "They brought a beautiful apple pie."

Elizabeth's eyes lit up. "Ummm, my favorite! When is Sara going to have her baby? It's taking forever!"

Jane laughed. "I think Sara would agree with you there." Just then, Jane remembered the dough she'd left rising in the kitchen. "Oh, my! I forgot about my bread. It's probably halfway to the ceiling by now."

Elizabeth followed Jane to the kitchen where the dough was found to be salvageable once she punched it down. Jane prepared the bread to bake then fixed a simple lunch for herself and Elizabeth. Luke had packed a lunch again, so Jane knew he wouldn't be back until suppertime.

The familiar aroma of yeast filled the house as the bread baked, but the afternoon heat combined with the stove's heat and compelled Jane to spend the rest of the day tending the garden. Elizabeth helped, and together they were able to finish the weeding she had started yesterday.

After washing up by the pump, Elizabeth and Jane changed their dirt-smudged dresses and began supper preparations. As she cooked, perspiration dripped from

Jane's face, and she repeatedly swiped her forehead with her arm. Shortly before they were finished, Luke appeared.

"Howdy, ladies." He stopped just short of the kitchen door. "It's hot as fire in here. What'd you do, cook all day?"

His smile took the sting from his words, but Jane was infuriated that he'd guessed correctly. She should have known better than to try and bake bread in the heat of the afternoon. Her mother had taught her better than that! Jane set the last platter on the table and pulled herself up straight. "In fact, that's just what I did, Mr. Reiley, do you have something to say about that?"

Jane saw Luke's mouth twitch, but to his credit, he was able to keep a straight face as he said, "Perhaps some fresh air would be nice," then he proceeded to prop open the front door.

Elizabeth and Jane took their seats as Luke made his way back to the table. Luke had no more than finished saying grace when they heard a horse coming full speed into the yard. Luke was the first to reach the porch, with Jane and Elizabeth shortly behind. Nathan McClain reared the horse to a stop in front of the house.

"What's wrong, Nathan?"

"It's Sara. The baby's coming." He was out of breath from the hard ride. "The pains are coming fast, and Hetty and Gus are at the Reverend Hill's for supper. She's all alone." He pinned Jane with a plea. "Please, Jane, you have to go to her. She asked me to send for you, then get Doc and Hetty."

Luke jumped in. "Why don't I get them, and you can take Jane back to your house."

"I don't want to waste time while you saddle a horse. She needs the doctor quick. I'm afraid something's wrong."

"All right. You go, and I'll take Jane to Sara."

Nathan rode off toward town, and Luke ran to the barn to saddle a horse. Jane stood in bewilderment. Why did Sara ask for her? She knew nothing about birthing babies! And Luke hadn't even given her a chance to speak for herself. What if she did something wrong? She'd only been six when her mother had given birth to Katy, and she'd been shooed from the house for the day. What if the baby came before Nathan returned with the doctor and Hetty?

"I hope Sara's going to be okay." Elizabeth's comment brought Jane to the present. Before she could comment, Luke rode over on a mammoth horse.

"Come here, Jane. You can ride in front of me."

He held out his hand, but Jane just stared in horror. She'd never even sat on one of the beasts.

"Come on, Jane!" The impatience, which edged his voice, propelled her forward. She stepped up to the horse, and Luke's hands circled her waist. She closed her eyes and gripped his hands as he settled her sidesaddle in front of him.

"Can't I come, too?" Elizabeth pleaded.

"Sorry, Sis. You stay here and look after the house for me, all right?"

Luke nudged the horse as Elizabeth nodded, disappointment dulling her eyes. *If only we could trade places!*

Before Jane could even finish her thought, the horse was off and running. Luke maintained the reins with his right hand and had his left arm firmly around Jane's waist. She clung to his arm with both hands and buried her face in his shoulder. They were wrapped so firmly together that their bodies moved as one on the horse.

 is

Luke guided his mount through the grove of trees and across the prairie grass. At first his mind was on Sara and the baby as he prayed earnestly that all would go well. To be alone and in such pain was bad enough, but what if she were to deliver the baby without help? Nathan had sensed that something was wrong, and he wasn't one to panic.

Luke was thankful he lived close to Nathan, but the ride seemed to be taking an interminable amount of time. Just then, he became aware of pain gripping his left arm. Looking down, he saw that Jane's arms were wrapped around his and her fingers were digging into his flesh. She'd turned her head into his chest, preventing Luke from viewing her face, but her clinging body made her terror obvious.

The fact that this abrasive woman had a vulnerable spot stunned him. He had often thought there was nothing that could shake her. Her impenetrable shell stood firm against anyone daring enough to converse with her. Even her posture and clothing reflected her harsh attitude. She wore only the drabbest colors, carried herself rigidly, and wore her hair scraped back into a tight roll. Just thinking about her hairstyle gave him a headache.

Yet here she was, clinging desperately to him. He tightened his hold around her waist, trying to make her feel more secure as their bodies jolted together on the saddle.

"It's all right," he said quietly. "We're almost there."

He maintained his firm hold, though his arm ached, and it was difficult to keep his balance. When the house came into sight, Luke slowed the horse. Jane released his arm gradually until she was sitting on her own accord. Luke dismounted, then held his arms up for Jane, who was visibly shaken.

As they mounted the porch steps, Luke prayed that Jane would be able to get hold of herself in time to help Sara. They entered the house, and Luke stopped at the bottom of the stairs as Jane ascended to the second story.

❧

Jane's legs trembled as she mounted the stairs. She'd never been in the McClain house before, but the quiet moans seemed to be coming from the first room to the left of the landing. She wished she had time to compose herself. First the ride, now this. She gritted her teeth and forced her mind to the task at hand.

The door to the bedroom gaped open, and Jane quickly surveyed the situation as she rushed over to Sara's side. The woman's face was twisted in a grimace of pain, and her throat emitted a primal groan. She was half-sitting on the bed, her upper body propped up by a mound of pillows. Her skirt was draped tentlike over her knees, which were drawn up toward her swollen belly.

Jane intuitively grasped Sara's hand, which was clutching a handful of quilt. Sara didn't acknowledge her presence, for she was too deep in her pain to even be aware of anything else.

When the pain subsided, Sara rolled her head on the pillow to face Jane. Her face was flushed with effort, and beads of perspiration dotted her forehead and upper lip.

"Oh, Jane! Thank God you're here!" she gasped. "I thought I was going to have this baby all by myself."

Jane put on what she hoped was a reassuring smile. "I'm here now. Everything's going to be just fine."

"I've been trying not to push for the last few pains, but it's getting almost impossible." The last words were released with a gush of air as her pains began again.

Sara's face slowly darkened to a deep red as she squeezed her eyes shut and ground her teeth together. Jane knew by the sound she released that she was bearing down.

Sara clasped her hand as she pushed. The pressure this small woman was exerting on her hand amazed Jane! Sara caught her breath and began bearing down again. Jane's mind worked furiously. What would she do if the baby came before the doctor arrived? She scanned the room for something she could use to wrap around the infant. A stack of folded bedding sat on top of the bureau. That would have to do. She also saw a pitcher and wash basin that would serve to bathe the baby.

The pressure on her hand began to let up, and she turned her thoughts back to Sara.

"I'm so glad you're here," Sara breathed.

Jane smiled and awkwardly patted her hand. *She wouldn't be so glad if she knew how inexperienced I am!*

"The water in the basin is fresh. I can't believe this is happening so fast! I just had a backache all day, and then my water broke at supper and. . ."

Sara drew a deep breath and began bearing down again. Jane covered their hands with her other one and murmured, "That's it. You're doing fine."

Once again, Jane began planning what to do next. She would put some bedding under Sara's hips to keep the quilt clean. Would there be blood? And what about the cord? What was she supposed to do about that?

Jane went to work when the pains let up, easing some cloths under Sara and arranging her skirts so she could see when the baby's head appeared.

A voice from downstairs diverted her attention. "Jane, is everything okay up there?"

"Everything is fine!" *Except I have no idea what I'm doing!*

Sara looked into Jane's eyes. "I don't think the doctor is going to make it."

"If he doesn't, then he just doesn't, that's all. We'll do it together. You and me."

Sara's faced relaxed in a smile before tensing up again as another contraction gripped her body. Every muscle was taut as Sara worked with all her power to bring her baby into the world.

"I can see the head!" A patch of black hair, about the size of a buckeye was showing. When Sara stopped pushing, the head retracted, and she could no longer see it. Sara caught her breath as Jane told her it wouldn't be long, now.

Sara was obviously buoyed by the knowledge that her baby would arrive soon.

With the next contraction, the head appeared once again. "You're doing great, Sara! I can see more of the head now." This contraction lasted longer than the others, and Sara drew a deep breath and pushed for the third time. She was progressing quickly, and Jane wondered if the next pain would yield the baby's head.

Sara relaxed as the contraction passed and smiled wearily at Jane. "How much can you see now?"

Jane touched her index fingers and thumbs together. "About this much. You might be able to get the head out on the next push."

"Doesn't look like the doctor's going to make it."

Jane thought she looked a little worried, so she tried to

reassure her. "God is in control." *Where did that come from?*

On the next contraction, Jane could see the baby's whole head, and she wondered that it didn't just pop out from all the pressure that Sara was exerting, but it wasn't until the one after that that the head finally glided out with a gush of blood and water.

"The head is out!" Jane used a corner of the bedding to wipe the mucus off the face and out of the mouth.

"Is he okay?" Sara asked.

"I think so. Now with the next pain, maybe his body will come out." Jane continued cleaning the baby's face with one hand, while supporting the head with the other.

Shortly after the next contraction began, the door downstairs slammed, and Jane heard the thundering of feet on the stairs. Her mind, however, was on the baby that slithered into her arms, warm and wet. "Oh, Sara!" Jane was overcome by the tiny slippery bundle.

Hetty and the doctor rushed into the room in time to see baby McClain slide into the world.

Sara tried to see the baby. "Is he okay?"

Just as the doctor rushed over to the baby, a loud cry filled the air. Everyone smiled and released a breath of relief.

Hetty grabbed Sara's hand as the doctor took the baby from Jane. "From the sounds of it, he's as feisty as his daddy!"

Jane joined the women at the head of the bed. "Actually, *she* is as feisty as her daddy!"

Sara and Hetty gaped at Jane and said simultaneously, "It's a girl?"

Jane nodded and smiled. "Oh, Sara, she's just beautiful!"

The doctor finished clamping the cord, and Hetty went to bathe the baby.

A voice from downstairs called, "Is everything all right up there?"

Jane walked to the open door and called down to Nathan, Luke, and Gus, who were gathered at the foot of the stairs. "Sara and the baby are fine! Nathan, you have a beautiful daughter."

"A girl! Did you here that, Luke? I have a daughter."

"You're happy now, but just you wait until the boys start callin' on her," Luke said.

Jane smiled, then went back into the bedroom and shut the door. Hetty finished bathing the baby, who did not appear to enjoy her first bath. The doctor continued to work with Sara, so Jane perched herself on the edge of the bed.

"I don't know how to thank you, Jane. I couldn't have done this without you."

"Nonsense. You were doing just fine by yourself."

Just then, Hetty brought the bundled baby over and handed her to Sara.

"Oh, just look at you!" Fresh tears filled the new mother's eyes as she gazed at her baby. The infant hushed upon hearing her mother's voice and stared at Sara wide-eyed.

The doctor stood and gathered his supplies. "Well, Mrs. McClain, looks like a perfectly healthy baby to me. I'm all through here. Hetty, if you'll get Mrs. McClain all cleaned up, I'll go and reassure the new papa. Miss Cooper, you did a fine job."

Jane smiled, and Hetty profusely apologized to Sara for not being with her during the labor. Sara insisted that everything was all right. After Sara was cleaned and put into her nightclothes, Jane and Hetty went downstairs to get Nathan. He quickly scaled the stairs to see his wife and new baby.

While Dr. Hathaway said his good-byes, Hetty prepared tea and cakes for her husband, Jane, and Luke. Jane, ravenous from having missed supper, had to restrain herself from devouring the cake, for fear of appearing gluttonous. Luke, however, had no such compunctions and freely attacked the food.

Nathan came down shortly afterward, and Hetty went back up to care for the baby while Sara rested. Jane was exhausted, and when Luke suggested they return home, she was more than agreeable. However, she'd forgotten their only means of transportation and stopped short when she saw the stallion tied loosely to a tree. Luke nearly plowed her down.

"Sorry!" he said when he collided with her.

The force of the impact sent her forward a step, but she abruptly gained control of herself and stiffened her spine. If he thought she was going to climb on that beast again, he should think again!

Luke couldn't have missed her hesitancy. "Want to race home and see if we can beat the time we set on the way here?"

Jane heard the laughter in his voice and knew without looking that a grin tugged at his lips. She crossed her arms, saying nothing as he stepped beside her. Leave it to him to find a weak spot and rub it in. Why did he insist on tormenting her?

To her surprise, Luke touched her chin and turned her face toward him. His eyes were twinkling with amusement, but his grin reflected compassion rather than ridicule. "I'll take it real slow, all right?"

She briskly nodded once, dislodging his hand, and walked rigidly to the stallion.

"Why don't you sit astride this time? You'll be able to balance better."

He hoisted her up to the saddle, and she swung her right leg over. The horse staggered to the side, and Jane grabbed the saddle horn with both hands. To be up so high on an unsteady horse was a frightening thing, and she was relieved when Luke pulled himself up behind her and draped an arm around her waist.

After nudging the mount with his foot, they set off at a slow pace. The ride was long compared to their earlier dash across the terrain, but she'd rather ride all night at this pace than be subjected to a repeat of their earlier harrowing experience. They arrived at the Reiley home without incident, and Jane immediately retired to her cottage.

That night as she laid in bed, her mind repeatedly reviewed the baby's delivery. She smiled in the dark, remembering the miniature hands and perfectly formed face. She was in awe of the whole process of child bearing, that two people could join together and create a new little life. How exciting it must be to see the little one that's a part of you and your spouse.

Jane had never truly thought about the fact that she would never have children of her own. Oh, she had known, of course, that since there would be no husband, there could be no children, but she had never allowed herself to consider what that meant. Suddenly, the life of a spinster seemed lonely and dismal.

Tears formed behind her eyelids as she allowed herself

to grieve the children she would never have. A part of her was envious of Sara, who had all the things Jane would never have. She was disgusted with herself for her begrudging thoughts.

If only God had made her differently! Why did she have to be the one who was ugly? The one with the long, spindly arms and legs, the unsightly freckles, and the homely features? And why did she have to be born into a family of beauties? That was the worst of it! She was plain by anyone's standards, but when held up next to her sisters, she stood out like a wart. She would never forget the taunting and teasing during her childhood that had humiliated her so. She learned very early that boys did not want to play with homely girls. When boys began calling on other girls her age, no one was less surprised than she that no one expressed an interest in her. Socials, parties, and hayrides only marked further humiliation for Jane as all the other girls received invitations and twittered about dresses and courting.

Jane had always been on the outside, excluded from the normal activities of young people, and too mortified to go to them unattended. She had been so preoccupied with just getting through those horrible years, that she hadn't fully realized the implications of spinsterhood.

In that moment, helping her parents in the restaurant didn't seem very fulfilling. In fact, the prospect seemed downright depressing. If only God had made her differently!

six

Jane woke in a sour mood the next day. During breakfast, Elizabeth chattered about Sara and the baby until Jane was ready to tell her to hush. She felt mean-spirited, and although she knew Elizabeth was merely excited, she didn't want to hear about babies today. Luke left her alone for a change, seeming to sense her bad mood.

Jane's critical attitude followed her to church, where she sat with her family. Luke had arranged for Jane to have Sundays off, so she planned to spend the afternoon with her family. The congregation rose and sat at the appropriate times, and Jane complied with the rituals without interest. As they rose for the reading of the Scriptures, Jane listened to the Reverend Hill, if only to occupy her mind.

"Today, we will look at Psalm 100, verses 3 and 4. 'Know ye that the Lord he is God: it is he that hath made us, and not we ourselves; we are his people, and the sheep of his pasture. Enter into his gates with thanksgiving, and into his courts with praise: be thankful unto him, and bless his name.' Let us pray."

Bitterness boiled up within Jane as she bowed her head. God *had* made her! She would not argue with that. He had made her ugly!

When Jane was a young girl, her mother had talked to her about Jesus, and she had asked Him into her heart that day. She remembered how carefree and naïve she'd been.

51

She had been old enough to understand what Jesus had done for her, but too young to know that her appearance would ruin her life. Some of the bitterness drained from her heart as sadness creeped in to take its place. She had given herself to God, but somewhere along the way, they had diverged, she and the Lord.

This was another way she was set apart from her family. Everyone else in her family seemed very close to God. Her mother was forever quoting Scripture. In fact, it was a joke amongst the Coopers that she had a verse for every occasion. Jane had always sensed her mother's disappointment in her lack of spiritual depth, although she had never said anything directly.

Jane startled from her reverie when those around her took their seats. She settled back against the hard pew, arranged her skirt, and let her mind wander. The service seemed long today, perhaps because of the stifling heat in the small chapel. A warm breeze, almost oppressive, wafted through the open windows, bringing in the thick vibrant fragrance of lilac. Women waved fans with hypnotic repetition, men shrugged out of their suitcoats, and children fidgeted while their parents warned them to be still.

Jane looked forward to the afternoon. She would take the noon meal with her family, go see how the restaurant was progressing, then take a nap in her own bed. Just thinking of her feather mattress made her sigh with contentment. The sound drew her father's attention, and Jane gave a small, sheepish smile and made an effort to focus on the sermon.

After the service, she went home with her family for a meal of fried chicken, mashed potatoes, green beans, and some of her mother's delicious buttermilk biscuits. Her plans to see the restaurant were delayed in favor of a nap once the food settled in her stomach, making her feel satiated and lazy.

She enjoyed being in her own room again. Although she typically shared the space with Katy, her sister had gone to a friend's home for the afternoon. Now, Jane relished the idea of a couple hours of solitude. Her bed felt every bit as good as she remembered and, before she had time to think anymore, she drifted off into the darkness of sleep.

The sound of feet clomping up the stairs woke her, and she opened her eyes to see Katy tiptoeing into the room.

Katy saw Jane's eyes open and whispered, "Sorry! Didn't mean to wake you."

"That's all right. What time is it?"

"Four o'clock." Katy rummaged around in her chest until she found what she was looking for. "David is downstairs reading. I think he's eager to take you over to the restaurant; he's so proud, you'd think he built the place all by himself. The plans are still on schedule. The restaurant and house portion should be finished by the beginning of August, and the boarding rooms ready to rent sometime in August or September."

"I can't believe how much has been done this week." Jane sat up and rubbed her eyes. "It's by far the biggest building in town."

"Wait'll you see the inside. I can hardly wait to put everything in place—the tables and lamps and all."

Katy prepared to leave the room, and Jane called to her, "Tell David I'll be ready in a few minutes."

Jane's hair had come loose, so she pulled it back and

washed her face. That done, she went downstairs to join her brother.

Since the building was on the other side of town and the afternoon heat was sweltering, they took the carriage. David caught her up on what they had done that week. He was clearly enthusiastic about carpentry, and Jane wondered if he should consider it for a trade. Her father probably assumed he would take an interest in the restaurant and inn, but she thought the rest of them could manage fine. Her father could handle the bookkeeping. Of course, Katy would get married sooner or later, but by then the business would probably be earning enough to warrant some paid help.

Jane had seen the structure that morning as she rode to church with Luke and Elizabeth, but now, as they pulled up to the front and alighted from the carriage, she was awestruck at its expansiveness. Their building was located between the Feed 'n' Seed and Dr. Hathaway's office. The size of the restaurant and inn dwarfed both buildings.

The restaurant occupied the lower floor, and the boarding rooms were located above it. The Coopers' new two-story house was attached to the right side of the business and was as large as the restaurant and inn combined.

Jane and David mounted the steps leading to a full-length porch. Glass panes had been installed the previous week, and Jane noted the large, central window on which she would paint the name of the establishment.

David opened the finely carved wood door and stepped aside, allowing Jane to precede him. The tangy scent of lumber hung in the hot, still air, but bright sunlight flooded through the windows that surrounded the dining room, giving an ethereal appearance to the empty room.

"Oh, David, it's wonderful! All the natural lighting is. . ."

"I know." He walked to the right and gestured to the unfinished wall. "Mama wants to paper all the walls in the dining room. I think she wants your input. She can't seem to decide on a pattern." He pointed to the opposite wall where a staircase ran up to the second story. "Mr. Evans is making a banister. He does beautiful work, and he agreed to make the tables and chairs, too. It's actually cheaper to have him make them than to order them from back east."

"Where's the kitchen?"

David laughed. "Figures that's what a woman wants to see!" He led her to an open doorway located on the far wall. "There's not much in here yet, but you can see there's plenty of space for preparations. That's where the stoves are going to be."

"What about cabinets?"

"We did have to order those. Mr. Evans said it would be all he could do to get the tables and chairs done on time. Mama told us what she wanted, and that's what we ordered."

Jane could see why her family was so excited over the new business and was glad she had something to look forward to once her work at the Reileys' was finished.

David took her upstairs next, which consisted of four boarding rooms and two water closets, which would have to be shared. Next he led her through the dining room to the door on the far wall. "This leads to our new house. It's almost finished."

He opened the connecting door, and Jane saw that the place was nearly ready for occupancy. Her parents planned to move into the house about a week before the restaurant opened. The downstairs consisted of a large parlor, a kitchen, a water closet, a dining room, and her parent's room. The walls were partially papered, a work in progress. She liked the large floral print in shades of fall foliage.

Jane followed David up the open stairway and, once at the top, Jane marveled at the size of the bedrooms. The room she would share with Katy loomed at the top of the staircase, and just beyond that was David's room, which was slightly smaller than the one she and Katy would share. After the tour was completed, they made their way back to the carriage, and David flicked the reins, setting the bays in motion.

Supper was well underway when they returned, so Jane helped her mother and Katy finish. Just a week ago, she had dreaded going to the Reileys' house, but tonight she just felt indifferent about going back. The assignment hadn't been so bad, really.

After supper, her father drove her back to the cottage that would be her home for the next three weeks. She wasn't the least bit tired, so she took out her art supplies and sketched from memory the inside of the restaurant's dining room. She added the linen-covered tables and empty chairs, a floral paper for the walls, and a delicately carved banister. When she was finished, she saw that it was a good representation, but the emptiness of the dining room left her feeling lonely.

❧

The next morning, Jane and Elizabeth fell into the familiar routine of the previous week. After Elizabeth milked the cows, she helped Jane prepare the morning meal. Elizabeth was still excited about Sara's new baby and wanted to know when they could go for a visit.

"I think today would be too soon. Perhaps tomorrow we'll bake and deliver them a cake." Her answer satisfied Elizabeth, who was eager to hold the newborn.

When Luke came in, they took their seats and said grace. While everyone filled their plates, Elizabeth chattered, and Luke teased like the big brother he was.

"Jane says we can go see the baby tomorrow, Luke. I can't wait!" She looked at Jane with a frown between her eyebrows. "Should we take something for the baby?"

"Perhaps." Jane had an idea. "I saw some spare material in a chest upstairs. Maybe we can make a bib or bonnet."

"Do you mean it? You'll help me?"

Jane was caught off guard by Elizabeth's enthusiasm, then remembered Elizabeth no longer had her mother. Jane's heart warmed toward the girl, and she gave her a genuine smile as she responded. "Of course I'll help you. We'll start on it after breakfast."

"Oh, thank you, Jane! I just love little baby things!" She paused to take a sip of milk. "I wonder when Caleb and Cassy will have a baby. I hope it'll be soon."

Elizabeth proceeded to eat, but Jane saw from the corner of her eye how Luke's fork paused between his plate and mouth before continuing on its way. She looked at him and, although his eyes were fixed on the table, she read the misery there. He continued eating, but his eyes looked hollow and a vein bulged in the middle of his forehead. How awful this must be for him. What would he do when Caleb and Cassy returned and he would have to face them every day?

Just then, as if he'd felt her eyes on him, his gaze darted up and he pierced her with his stare. His eyes held hers in an unseverable grip as intense seconds dragged. He seemed to be studying her, and Jane wondered if he had guessed she knew his feelings for Cassy. A slow flush bloomed along Luke's cheeks and, when he finally looked away, his chair grated across the floor, startling Jane.

He stood, leaving a half-empty plate, and shoved his hat on his head. "I won't be back for lunch," he mumbled before he strode across the room and out the door.

Elizabeth shattered the silence. "Boy, what's his problem? He's just not been himself lately."

Jane gave a small semblance of a smile and thought it best to change the subject. "I don't know, but if we're going to make something for the baby, we'd better get to work."

As she helped Elizabeth work on the bonnet, Jane couldn't get Luke off her mind. He'd looked so sad. With Luke, it was easy to forget there was a vulnerable being inside his happy-go-lucky shell. He was forever teasing and laughing in a way that was distinctly Luke and, although he irritated her many times, she realized he didn't mean any harm. She resolved to be more careful of his feelings in the future. After all, he was only human.

❧

Luke strode out of the barn, slamming the crude door harder than he intended. As he saddled Ginger, his mind drifted back to breakfast. Elizabeth's innocent comment about Caleb and Cassy having a baby had slammed into him like a fist into his gut, almost knocking the breath from him. It's not that he hadn't thought of it before. But for some reason hearing Elizabeth say it had made it seem all the more real.

The crazy thing was, his feelings for Cassy seemed

blurred, as if distance had obscured his feelings. He wondered at this and admitted he didn't understand what was happening in his heart. She'd only been gone a week.

He hadn't known what to think when he'd caught Jane staring at him. To find her looking at him at all was out of character. Then to catch her feeling sorry for him—and he was sure that's what she was doing—was disconcerting and humiliating. Had she guessed his feelings for Cassy? He'd been so careful to hide them, yet what other reason would she have to pity him?

Luke mounted Ginger and nudged her to a gallop. He'd best get his mind on ranch business, or he'd never get anything done.

≥∙

That evening after supper, Jane pulled the Boston rocker onto the cottage's small front porch in hopes of enjoying the best part of the warm July day. Summer's heat now attacked the region with vigor, and only the shade of a large tree or a fresh breeze gave a body relief.

A copse of trees directly ahead framed the setting sun, and the brilliant pink and purple slashes inspired the artist in her. So, what began as a rest turned into a painting session. Pulling another chair from the house, she put it in front of the rocker to use as a makeshift easel. She worked quickly, knowing how fast the colors would fade once the sun sank below the horizon.

She used her dry brush to softly blend the colors together. The blazing sunset silhouetted the trees, and she knew her time was almost up. She was so absorbed in her work that she didn't hear Luke approaching until he was almost upon her.

"Enjoying the view?"

Her brush sliced across the painting, streaking the canvas with a violet strand. Jane huffed. "Now see what you've done?"

Luke approached, viewing the piece. "Real sorry about that, Jane. I thought you heard me coming." To his credit, he sounded repentant.

Upon hearing his apology, Jane relented and used a cloth to wipe away as much as possible.

"Will you be able to fix it?"

Jane gave a curt nod. "With time."

"Elizabeth told me you were an artist, but I had no idea you were so good."

Jane shifted in her seat, wondering what she was supposed to say. When nothing occurred to her, she remained quiet and began to repair the painting. Luke watched over her shoulder, making her terribly conscious of every brush stroke. Her steady hand began to shake as her nerves grew taut. Didn't the man know painting was not a spectator sport? She worked as quickly as she could to cover the faint purple stain, but she grew clumsier with each passing minute, until finally she'd had it.

"Is there something you wanted, Luke?" she asked, exasperation coating every word.

She heard the smile in his voice. "Why, Jane, am I making you nervous?"

"Of course not." She set her jaw and continued working, more to avoid his eyes than anything.

"You *are* nervous. Why does it bother you for people to watch you paint?"

"Not *people,* just you," she retorted without thinking.

"*I* make you nervous?" He chuckled in disbelief. "So, now I know two things that make you nervous."

Jane paused long enough to send him an irritated glance. "What are you talking about?"

"Horses, of course." Luke moved to the porch rail and leaned insolently against it with his arms crossed smugly in front of his body.

His arrogant pose made Jane's blood boil. "First of all, if you think I'm intimidated by you, you're just. . .wrong, and secondly, I am *not* afraid of horses!"

Luke threw his head back and laughed as if amused by her denial.

"I'm not!" she reiterated.

It seemed to take a great effort on Luke's part to regain control and, even then, he was unable to prevent his lips from twitching. "So, you're not afraid of horses, is that right?"

"Of course I'm not afraid," Jane stated with confidence.

"Well, I'm right glad to hear that, Jane, 'cause I just came over to see if you wanted to take a little ride."

Jane's brush froze in midair. "A ride?"

"Uh-huh, I thought you might like to see more of the ranch. I have just the right horse for you." Luke's mouth continued to twitch, and his eyes challenged hers.

Jane fought for an excuse and, like magic, her mind emptied.

"Chicken?" Luke asked with quiet emphasis as he hiked a brow.

Jane bristled. "Why, of all the nerve! You, Mr. Reiley, are the most obnoxious, rude man I have ever met. Furthermore, just because I have no training in horse riding does not mean I am afraid. I. . .I just don't know how to ride, that's all. And I might add that it's extremely ungentlemanly of you to call it to my attention." When, after all of Jane's insults, Luke only looked more amused, Jane stopped her tirade and began snatching up her supplies.

"Whoa there, little lady." Luke gripped her arm to stop her frenzy, and she stared at his hand with barely contained outrage until he released her. "I'm glad we've cleared up this little problem," he said, his face teeming with amusement. "See, I thought you were afraid of horses, and now I find out you're just untrained. That's a different thing altogether."

Jane stared at him, dumbfounded at having made him see her way. "Well. . .I'm glad you see how things are."

"Oh, I do. Training is simple to remedy. All you need are lessons. And since you have been so kind as to fill in for Esther while she's away, I insist that you let me provide those lessons." Luke pulled himself up to his full height, his eyes twinkling in the dusky light.

"Oh, but I. . ."

"I insist, Jane." Luke tipped his hat and began walking to his house.

"Mr. Reiley, really. . ."

"We'll start tomorrow evenin', Jane," he tossed over his shoulder. "Be sure to wear a full skirt so you can ride astride." Luke vaulted up the porch steps and disappeared into his house.

Oh, for heaven's sake! How was she supposed to get out of this? Jane plucked her canvas off the chair and stomped into the house.

seven

The next day, following breakfast, Jane made two teacakes while Elizabeth worked on the baby's gift. While the cakes baked, Jane helped Elizabeth with the eyelet ruffle that would rim the bonnet, then she showed her how to run the satin ribbon through the border.

Elizabeth had already known the sewing basics, and Jane was surprised at how quickly the girl learned. After this project, she was sure Elizabeth would be able to fashion a bonnet all by herself, and she told Elizabeth so.

The tiny hat was completed shortly after the cakes had finished baking and, when they had cooled, Jane draped a cheesecloth across one of the pans and set the other aside for supper, before starting off toward the McClain ranch.

The midmorning temperature was already elevated, but the sunbonnets that shielded their faces and the steady breeze that flowed by them atop the buckboard allowed some degree of comfort.

The baby bonnet, nestled in brown wrapping paper and tied with a piece of string, was cradled carefully in Elizabeth's arms, as if she were holding the baby herself. It had been rewarding to help her with the gift and even more rewarding to see how proud she was of her effort.

When they drove up to the house, they immediately spotted Hetty, who was on her knees tending the garden out back. Upon seeing them, Hetty pulled herself to her feet and walked toward them waving.

After Jane reined in the horses, she alighted from the wagon, then helped Elizabeth down behind her.

"Hello, Jane and Elizabeth. Land sakes, I'm a filthy mess!" she exclaimed as she dusted off her skirts. "Don't reckon it makes much difference, anyway, since I'm sure you didn't come to see me. Come on in, and I'll pour you a nice, cool glass of lemonade."

Jane and Elizabeth followed her into the house where Sara rocked the infant. Jane handed the cake over to Hetty, who thanked her graciously, then disappeared into the kitchen.

Sara smiled a welcome. "Hello, Jane. Elizabeth. How kind of you to come and bring a cake."

Elizabeth tentatively approached and held out her gift. "We brought the baby a present, too. I made it!" She glanced sheepishly at Jane. "I mean Jane and I made it."

"Elizabeth did the work. I just showed her what to do," Jane said.

"Well! How thoughtful." Sara rose to her feet as the baby made little gurgling noises. "Elizabeth, would you like to hold Caroline while I open the present?"

The girl's eyes widened with delight. "Oh! May I?"

"Of course you may. Here, sit in the rocker, and I'll hand her to you."

Elizabeth did as she asked, and seconds later she was cradling the newborn. "She's so tiny! Look at her little fingers!"

Sara smiled at the wonder in Elizabeth's voice. "Please have a seat, Jane. I can hardly believe it was just three days ago that you were helping me deliver her." The two women seated themselves on the settee. "I don't know what I would have done without you."

"Don't be silly. I really didn't do anything."

"Just having you there was such a comfort. God sure was watching out for me. I nearly had the baby alone."

Jane shifted in her seat, unsure what to say next.

Elizabeth filled the gap. "Open the present, Mrs. McClain!"

Sara untied the twine and opened the lumpy package. "Oh, how precious! A little bonnet." She fingered the lace trim and examined the tiny stitches. "You're quite a fine seamstress, Elizabeth. And it looks like you had a proficient teacher." She smiled at Jane. "Thank you so much. I think I'll have her wear this to her first Sunday service."

Elizabeth beamed. "Oh, Jane, you just have to hold Caroline!"

"Well. . .I suppose I could." When Jane made no move to get up, Sara stood and gathered Caroline, then put the baby in Jane's arms. Miniature blue eyes gazed unblinkingly at Jane. Her cheeks had filled out some since her delivery, and her skin had blossomed to a delicate pink. "She's just beautiful, Sara."

"Thank you. God has blessed us."

"Amen to that!" Hetty declared as she entered with a tray of drinks, sandwiches, and slices of the teacake. "Jane and Elizabeth brought the cake, Sara. Thought I'd serve it now since it looks so good."

Sara took a piece of cake off the tray and delicately took a bite. "It's delicious, Jane."

"Thank you." Little Caroline was still gazing into Jane's eyes. What would it be like to have your own baby? To have a part of you and the man you love rolled into a precious little bundle. Jane had never been the nurturing type, but the thought of having her own child to care for made her stomach flutter with excitement. It would be so wonderful to have a child to take care of. To mold into a unique individual. The baby gurgled just then and twisted her face into a contortion of distress before letting loose a tiny squeal.

Sara set her glass down and reached over to take the baby. "I'm afraid she's hungry again. That's all she seems to do is eat."

"Well, she's gotta eat if she's gonna grow." Hetty held out the tray for Jane. "Have a sandwich and cake, Jane."

Jane helped herself now that her arms were free. The sandwich was delicious and filling, and she was pleased that the cake had turned out well: moist and bursting with flavor.

Caroline had quieted as Sara discreetly fed her. The women chatted for a short while, but when the infant drifted off to sleep, Jane thought it prudent to let the new mother rest, so she and Elizabeth said good-bye.

Elizabeth talked about the baby all the way home. It was clear that she yearned for a little baby in the way that young girls frequently do. Her thoughts were immature and romantic, giving no consideration to the hours of work and endless nights of crying that a child brings. Jane smiled to herself, but didn't say anything to Elizabeth about her idyllic dreams.

As the girl prattled on about babies, Jane's mind unwittingly began to wander. She found herself lost in her own dreams that involved her own house to keep and children to care for. She was mentally singing nursery songs to her own little baby when she realized Elizabeth was calling her name.

"I'm sorry, did you say something?"

Elizabeth laughed. "I just asked if you'd like to marry someday."

The question revived her like a slap in the face. "For now, I'm planning to help my parents with their restaurant. With Cassy gone, they'll need my help." She was glad to be turning into the Reiley drive. With any luck, Elizabeth would drop the subject.

A hollow ache settled in Jane's stomach. Here she'd been dreaming of children and a family of her own when there was not a man anywhere who would take her as his wife. Why, her dreams were every bit as silly as Elizabeth's. Sillier, even. After all, at least part of Elizabeth's dreams would come true. She was a comely girl, and soon boys would be swarming around her. She would have a husband and children one day. Of course, they wouldn't lay contentedly in her arms all day the way she imagined, but her dreams were closer to reality than Jane's had been.

She would be more careful in her thinking from now on. There was no point wishing for something that would never be.

⁂

The remaining hours of the afternoon dragged. She worked around the house and used her thought time trying to come up with a reasonable excuse to forgo the riding lessons. Everything she invented sounded lame at best and chicken-hearted at worst. She would not allow that man to think she was too afraid to try.

Oh, but she was dreading those lessons. The thought of sitting atop one of Luke's mammoth horses made her legs quake, and she wondered if he'd make fun of her fears. Jane wasn't sure which she dreaded the most: the horse or

Luke. There was no getting out of it. She'd just have to make herself do it for dignity's sake.

After Luke arrived home and supper began, Jane's taut muscles began to relax. They were nearly ready for dessert, and Luke hadn't mentioned the lessons at all. Here she'd been worked up about it all day, and Luke had forgotten. Why, his challenge last night had been no more than a little game designed to prove his point. She should be angry with him, but, in truth, she was so relieved that her spirits lightened considerably. She practically glided into the kitchen to retrieve the cake she had baked that morning.

The dessert was a success if lack of leftovers was any indication, and Jane was feeling especially triumphant as she stood to clear away the dishes. Elizabeth had started washing them, and Jane had returned to the table for the second time when Luke scooted his chair back with a grate. "I'll go ahead and saddle up your horse. Meet me at the stables when you're through here."

Jane's mouth dropped open, and her spirits collapsed. Luke had already turned to go, and as a last resort she heard herself utter, "But. . ." Nothing else came, just the one word. Yet, as Luke turned to look at her over his shoulder, she saw that it was enough. He saw her cowardice, and his eyes twinkled as he gave her his half-grin. "Didn't we agree on lessons tonight, Jane? I thought you'd be looking forward to it."

The challenge was there in his voice, almost tangible, and Jane's spine stiffened involuntarily. She had just drawn a deep breath, ready to fling false words of intention, when Elizabeth peeked out the kitchen door. "Are you really going to give her lessons, Luke?" She continued without pause. "Oh, can I watch? Please?" She drew out the word to at least two syllables.

Jane watched Luke in horror, silently begging him to prevent Elizabeth from witnessing her humiliation. Luke paid her no attention, but to her relief, he denied his sister's request. "Actually, I told Mr. Lindsey I'd send you over with some tools he needs to borrow."

"Aww, Luke. . ."

"Now, no talking back. I thought you might like to stay over there awhile and play with Mary."

Elizabeth perked up at that piece of information. "May I?"

"I don't see why not. Just help Jane finish up the dishes first."

Elizabeth scooted into the kitchen with new purpose, and Luke strode out the door as if all matters were settled.

The dishes were cleaned too quickly for Jane, but Elizabeth, excited about visiting her friend, had no more hung the towel on a peg than she said a quick good-bye and darted out to the stables to collect the tools.

Jane stalled, rearranging dishes and cleaning surfaces that were already spotless. Only when she had delayed the inevitable for as long as possible did she remove her apron and wander out to the stable. Luke had finished saddling a chestnut brown horse and was leaning on the split rail fence with lazy indolence, watching her approach. The sun was at his back, leaving his face in shadow, but when he spoke she heard the laughter in his voice.

"Thought you might be waiting for the moon to rise."

Jane crossed her arms as she drew to a halt a safe distance from both the horse and Luke. "I'll have you know that women's chores are much more time-consuming than a man would ever believe."

"Oh, I don't doubt that for a minute," he said as he turned toward her, exposing his taunting expression. "But Elizabeth, who I might add has been gone a good fifteen minutes, assured me that the kitchen was set to rights when she left."

Jane opened her mouth and ordered her mind to come up with some reasonable excuse, but Luke stepped in, relieving her empty mind of its task.

"Come on over and meet Brownie." Luke swaggered over to the horse and took the reins as Jane cautiously approached. "Go ahead and touch her. Let her get used to you. We've had Brownie a long time, and I can tell you she's the gentlest horse I've ever seen. Very predictable. Won't do anything you don't tell her to do."

Jane reached up to stroke Brownie's neck. Now that she was close, she saw that the horse was huge. She had hoped that Luke would choose a small horse for her, not this massive figure of a beast. She may be gentle, and that remained to be seen, but Jane was unsure if she could even mount the creature. The stirrups hung only to her waist. Even if she could get her foot that high, she was sure she couldn't do so without appearing unladylike. Besides that, the saddle didn't look big enough to accommodate both of them. Of course, they'd somehow managed on that harrowing ride to the McClains, but surely they made larger saddles than this.

Luke stepped up in front of her and clasped his hands together. "Here, I'll give you a leg up, then you can guide Brownie to the training area over there."

"By myself?" Jane blurted.

Luke's eyebrows darted skyward. "You expected me to ride with you?"

"Well, I just thought. . .that is, until I get used to the horse. . ."

Luke's lip twitched in that infuriating way it always did when she amused him. "Fine, Jane. But you still need to mount first. Just put your left foot in my hands and swing your other leg around the horse."

Luke's hands were cupped for her foot, and he bent his knees until he was low enough to assist her. Jane lifted her foot to Luke's hands while trying to remain steady on her other foot. Desperate to catch her balance, she clutched onto Luke's shoulders and looked into his face, which, she was surprised to see, was only inches from her own. "Are you trying to mount me or the horse? 'Cause if you're trying to mount the horse, I suggest you grab the saddle horn."

If it were possible for Jane to blush, she knew her face would be a fiery shade of red just about now. However, since she had never been able to do even *that* right, she simply huffed, "I know that, Mr. Reiley. I simply lost my balance." She transferred her hands to the appropriate spot and, before she could regain her equilibrium, Luke boosted her up. She found herself sitting higher than any human being had a right to be.

Luke adjusted the stirrups and attempted to slip her foot into it, but since her knees were clamped tightly around the horse, her foot didn't budge.

"Jane, you're squeezing the life out of Brownie. Just let your legs hang down."

Jane made a concerted effort to relax her leg muscles and found, to her relief, that she still maintained her precarious balance.

"That's better." Luke slipped her boot into the stirrup,

then rounded the horse to adjust the other side. When he was done, he removed her foot from the stirrup, inserted his own, and grabbed for the saddle horn. Jane jerked her hands out from under his, but when he mounted, the saddle slid sideways with a creak, and Jane grasped his hand in panic. In the next moment, Luke was seated behind her. He reached for the reins, and Jane reclaimed the saddle horn.

"You can't hold that thing the whole time, you know," Luke said with a smile in his voice. "Here, take the reins."

Jane received them, and Luke's hands fell to his thighs.

"Now, when you want her to go, just nudge her with your heel. Use the reins to guide her. If you want to go left, just tug on the left side of the rein. I'm gonna let you give all the commands. I'm just along for the ride."

Jane listened to the instruction and, when it ended, she took a deep breath and told her leg to give a nudge. It hung like a dead weight, ignoring her command. She felt her heart thudding in her chest and wondered if Luke could feel the pounding through her back.

The loose hair around her nape fluttered as he spoke. "The sun is setting, Jane." His laughing voice grated across her mind, giving her the gumption to act. One nudge later and Brownie was walking at a slow pace across the packed earth.

"Great. Now relax your muscles. Let your elbows hang down at your sides and loosen your grip on the reins."

Jane did as he instructed, then tugged on the right side of the strap to guide Brownie through the gate that led to the training area.

"Stay near the fence and practice guiding her in a circle. We won't do anything fancy tonight. I just want you to get comfortable."

Normally, Jane would have retorted, but just the tasks of guiding Browning and staying relaxed required all her concentration.

After several times around the circle, the guiding seemed more automatic, and she felt almost at ease about sitting atop the horse. As she relaxed, she became aware of other things. Like Luke's thighs pressing against the back of hers and his chest brushing her back. Her hips were cradled between his legs, and they rocked together to the rhythmic motion of the horse. She felt her ears burning at the thought and wondered if Luke was as aware of their position as she was.

"Are you plannin' to scale that wall?"

Jane snapped to and realized Brownie had come to a halt at the wall of the stable. She had been so distracted she had forgotten to guide the horse around the circle.

Jane stiffened her spine and guided Brownie back to the circle. "Must you always be so impertinent?"

"She speaks! I was beginning to wonder."

Jane let his comment go, not wanting to justify it with a remark.

She led Brownie around the circle again and again until her back was beginning to ache. Luke must have noticed her squirming in the saddle.

"I think that's enough for today. Just guide her over to the front of the stable."

Jane did as he asked, then gave the reins a tug when the horse drew near the stable. She was pleased with how comfortable she was feeling now. The height didn't really bother her much, and she was already used to the swaying of the horse.

Jane dropped the reins and waited for Luke to dismount.

He grabbed the saddle horn and swung his leg behind him, but as he did so the saddle tilted unexpectedly, and Jane, who wasn't holding on, tilted with it.

The fall seemed to happen in slow motion. Luke was caught off-balance, having one foot still in the stirrup and the other only halfway to the ground. Jane frantically grabbed at Luke's arm, which was firmly attached to the saddle horn. His downward momentum combined with her sudden tilt to bring them both to the ground with a thud.

Luke grunted as Jane's weight hit him full in the stomach, then a moment of stunned silence ensued.

Jane opened her eyes and discovered she was on her side and on top of Luke. She pushed up on her elbows and, much to her horror, saw that her chest was level with Luke's eyes. She scrambled to a sitting position in the dirt.

Luke blinked as if trying to get his bearings, then turned his head sideways. "You all right?"

She began brushing the dust from her sleeves. "I'm fine. And you?"

Luke sat up beside her and ran his hand through his hair. "I think I'm still in one piece."

Jane paused and looked at Luke. Sure enough, it was there. A twitching grin was ready to give way to full-bodied laughter. Almost before she completed the thought, his laughter burst forth as he tipped his face skyward and flung his arm across his stomach, emitting rich, loud guffaws.

Jane sat gaping at him, wondering how this man always found something to laugh at, no matter the occasion. Just then, he turned to look at her with crinkly eyes and a wide boyish grin. "You have to admit, Jane," he said in between chuckles, "we must have been quite a sight!"

Jane reviewed the episode in her mind, seeing it from a spectator's view. All of her gangly limbs clutching at Luke as he went off-balance. A reluctant grin tugged at the corners of her mouth, which she quickly tried to suppress by pursing her lips.

"Well, I'll be hornswoggled. . .if that isn't a real smile," Luke said in wonder.

Having lost the battle of the smile, Jane ducked her head in an effort to hide her amusement.

Luke tipped her chin up with a finger, and Jane saw that his face was a mask of serious contemplation, although his eyes were still alight with humor. "You know, I think for your next lesson we shall cover the rudiments of a proper dismount." His face gave way to laughter, and Jane found her own face breaking loose in a smile as she breathed a quiet laugh.

As Luke's laughter faded away, Jane glanced up. His gaze bore into hers with intense speculation. "What?" she asked, the remnant of a smile still lingering on her face.

"I've never seen you like this," he said, smiling. "Your face all lit up and your eyes sparkling. . ."

She squirmed and resumed the task of brushing off her skirt. "My eyes do not sparkle."

"Yes they do. They have little gold flecks that sparkle when you smile."

"Don't be silly." Jane began picking imaginary lint from her dress. "They're plain old brown, just like. . ." Jane stopped short of completing the sentence, which would have sounded rude.

Luke cocked a brow, and his mouth tilted in a grin. "Just like mine?"

Jane stood to her feet, stiffening her spine as she continued dusting the dirt from her backside. "I didn't say that!" Why was this infuriating man always putting words in her mouth? Making her squirm purely for his own entertainment. "I just meant they're ordinary brown, not an unusual color, like Cassy's." She paused for effect. "But I'm sure you've noticed that."

Jane watched Luke as her words sank in. The smile slid slowly from his face, and he narrowed his eyes as if trying to read her. She ducked her head again, this time in shame, as she realized what she'd done.

She heard, more than saw, Luke rise to his feet and retrieve his hat. When he turned to face her, she gathered the courage to meet his eyes.

"So," he said, "you know." He shoved his hands in his pockets and shuffled his feet, drawing an imaginary line in the dirt. His eyes studied the ground as a red flush climbed his neck.

His words formed a statement, rather than a question. Unwittingly, Jane had revealed her knowledge about his feelings for Cassy. She stood there, wishing she could find the words to smooth this over. Her eyes darted around the yard, and she caught brief glimpses of Luke whenever she dared.

Finally Luke spoke. "I thought I'd hidden my affections well." His feet suddenly stilled, and his head shot up, his wide eyes meeting hers. "Cassy doesn't—"

"No!" Jane exclaimed quickly, wanting to ease his suffering. "No. Cassy knows nothing."

Luke's eyes closed momentarily, then opened them to stare at a point near Jane's feet as he released a puff of pent-up breath. His features taut, he looked so serious and sad that Jane thought he almost looked like a different man. Luke, without his smile and twinkling eyes, just wasn't Luke at all. She had reminded him of something he wanted to forget and had shamed him by revealing her knowledge of the situation. The flush of his skin told of his humiliation.

Prickling heat flared up within Jane, starting at her stomach and moving outward through her limbs. How selfish she had been to fling out those words in a moment of retribution! What kind of woman was she to open up his wound deliberately? She searched her mind for something to say, something healing and kind.

Luke interrupted her thoughts. "How long have you known?" His eyes darted to hers, then back to the ground.

Jane cleared her throat. "Since the day of the wedding. When they were leaving. . .I saw your face." Luke nodded his head. Jane had never been good with words, much less apologies, but she knew she owed him one. "I'm very sorry for what I said. My words were cruel and, if I had stopped to think, I never would have said them. Your feelings are none of my concern."

Luke raised the corners of his lips in a semblance of a smile. "You didn't do anything wrong. The problem is mine."

Luke started for Brownie and began guiding her to the stable. "Don't give it another thought. I'll see you in the morning."

Jane made a hasty exit, eager to escape his presence. As she walked the short distance to the cottage, she berated herself for letting her nasty temper have its way.

૨ન

Luke unsaddled Brownie mechanically, reviewing his

conversation with Jane. He was ashamed, now as never before, that someone else knew. And why did that someone have to be Cassy's own sister? Besides Caleb or Cassy, Jane was the last person he would want to know his secret.

No wonder she'd been so terse with him. How could she respect him when he loved his own brother's wife? Even he couldn't respect himself.

Luke felt his face growing warm as he realized anew that Jane was aware of his feelings for Cassy. He felt naked, having his deepest, most secret feelings laid open before Jane.

He was as low as a worm. He knew it, and she did, too. The thought of facing her again was enough to make him squirm. At least she wouldn't bring the matter up again. He could tell she'd felt guilty about bringing up Cassy's name in the first place. She'd even gone so far as to apologize, which had surprised him to no end. In fact, Jane had dealt him two surprises tonight.

Luke's mouth unconsciously formed a smile as he reviewed their little mishap with the dismount. He had half-expected Jane to come stiffly to her feet and proclaim he was a clumsy oaf for dragging her to the ground in such a manner.

But to his surprise, she'd actually smiled. Not just a half-hearted grin, but a full-fledged, teeth-baring smile that had knocked him off his feet. Somewhere under that stern, brittle exterior was a woman he wanted to get to know. In fact, he would consider it a personal challenge to draw out the lighter side of Jane Cooper.

eight

The next day, the sun rose white-hot on a backdrop of clear blue. The air was still except for an occasional warm wind. By midmorning, Jane knew the day would be the hottest she had seen in Cedar Springs. She was grateful to be working outside in the shade, for the house was stuffy and oppressive already.

As she ran one of Luke's shirts through the wringer, she thought back to breakfast. Jane had dreaded seeing Luke again after their uncomfortable conversation the night before. During breakfast preparations, she had worried about what Luke would say and how he would act toward her.

Her worries were inflated, however, for after an initial flush, Luke proceeded to act as he always did, joking with Elizabeth and taunting Jane. Evidently, he had overcome the embarrassment of last night's exchange. Jane was glad for this, not only because she regretted her words, but also because she didn't want any further strain on her relationship with Luke. She still had to live here for another two weeks, after all.

Luke faced rough days ahead, and Jane wondered how he would cope once Cassy and Caleb returned. She didn't envy him. Surely, to never love at all would be better than to love someone who didn't return your love—much less your own brother's wife. She would have to be careful not to even hint of his feelings to Cassy. Her sister would feel horribly responsible if she knew of Luke's feelings. Of course, it wasn't her fault, but her sister was very sensitive to other people's feelings.

Jane heard a giggle and looked up to see Elizabeth standing in front of her. "Jane, you've been wringing that shirt for five minutes!"

Jane looked down at the shirt she'd been working on, then gave a laugh of her own. "I guess you're right. My mind was someplace else."

"Well, my mind is here, but I wish my body were someplace else! Like the creek, for instance! It's too hot to work today!"

Jane handed the shirt to Elizabeth, who proceeded to hang it on the line with the others. "Hot or cold, there's always work to be done."

"Do you think maybe we could go wading after lunch? We'll be done with the wash then."

Jane wiped the sweat off her face with the back of her hand. "I suppose we could. There's nothing else pressing to be done."

That news seemed to put a bounce in Elizabeth's step for the rest of the morning. In fact, even Jane was looking forward to dipping her feet into the cool water.

Jane and Elizabeth ate lunch on the porch to avoid the suffocating heat inside the house. The meal of cheese, apples, and bread allowed them to eat without having to use the stove. After a quick cleanup, they checked the clothes on the line and found them dry. Elizabeth assisted in folding and storing the clothes and linen, eager to head off for the creek.

When Jane proclaimed that all the work was done,

Elizabeth responded with animated glee, then led the way through the prairie grass toward the creek.

The walk was longer than Jane anticipated, and she was glad for her light-colored bonnet and dress. Eventually, she heard the trickling that indicated their arrival at the creek. Cottonwoods and willow trees lined the shallow creek bed, their heavy limbs providing a glorious reprieve from the sun.

Jane removed her bonnet, then sat in the tall grass to tug off her boots. Elizabeth was already dipping a toe into the bubbling water.

"Oh, Jane, water has never felt so wonderful!" Elizabeth stepped into the stream with both feet.

Jane finished peeling off her stockings and tiptoed to the bank feeling like a child. Elizabeth was knee-deep in the middle of the narrow creek when Jane pulled her skirt through her legs and tucked it into her waistband. She waded into the sun-speckled water, closing her eyes in ecstasy as the cool water rippled over her knees.

"Didn't I tell you this would be wonderful? I only wish the creek was deeper so I could jump in and get wet clear up to my neck!"

"Well, I can't make the water deeper, but I think I can help you out a little." Jane reached into the creek and brought up a cupful of water, slinging it toward Elizabeth. It was only a little water, so that barely a few drops fell onto the girl's pinafore, but she delighted in the play.

After a surprised laugh, Elizabeth sent a small spray of water back to Jane.

ða

Luke could hardly bear the incredible heat. Perspiration

soaked his clothes and, beneath his favorite tan hat, his hair was plastered to his head. Luke nudged Gretyl onward and swept away the rivulets that trickled down his face. He lifted his canteen from his saddlebag and drew it to his lips for a drink. However, he found the container nearly empty. Thankfully, he wasn't far from the creek where he could replenish his supply.

When the trees that lined the creek came into view, Gretyl quickened her pace as if she smelled the nearby water. "Got a thirst, do you, girl?" Luke asked as he patted her side.

As he neared the willows, Luke heard voices. He reined in Gretyl, pulling her to a stop just behind the huge, feathery willow branches. Luke peered through the foliage, wondering who was in his creek.

A grin pulled at Luke's mouth when he caught sight of Elizabeth wading in the center of the creek. He had just straightened and was about to advance when he heard Elizabeth address Jane. Luke glimpsed through the branches again, and a moment later Jane came into view. Her back was to him, and he was surprised to see she was only a dozen or so feet away.

Jane hiked her skirt up to her knees, and Luke turned away, certain that Jane would not appreciate having an uninvited spectator. After hearing the telltale splash of water, he looked back to see that Jane was standing knee-deep in the water. She and Elizabeth exchanged words, which he couldn't hear, then Jane shocked him by splashing water at Elizabeth.

The younger girl retaliated in kind and, within moments, Luke was witnessing an all-out water war. If he hadn't seen it, he never would have believed that Jane could be so playful. Why, it was only yesterday that he'd seen her smile for the first time. The laughter and squealing from both girls held his attention, and he found himself laughing at their antics as they frolicked in the water.

Eager to join the fun, Luke urged Gretyl forward and led her to the edge of the water. Elizabeth and Jane were so caught up in their game, they didn't see Luke until he spoke. "So this is what you two do all day while I'm working."

Their hands stopped midair, and Luke was almost surprised the water they were spraying didn't freeze in midair, too. The expressions on their faces were comical and induced a laugh from Luke. Elizabeth recouped quickly.

"Come join us, Luke! We're having a grand time!"

"I can see that." Luke saw that Jane was looking a bit embarrassed at having been caught playing like a child, so Luke decided to tease her. "Well, I'll come in, but only if Jane can control herself. I can see she's the best splasher around these parts."

Jane ducked her head, but not before Luke saw the beginnings of a smile. Dark spots speckled the bodice of her dress where water had splotched her, and her skirts had come loose, ballooning around her legs.

Luke tugged off his boots, then tied Gretyl near the stream so she could quench her thirst. After rolling up his pants, he walked to the water's edge.

❧

Jane watched as Luke splashed into the water, giving no thought to the rough fragments of rock that lined the bottom of the creek bed. Their eyes met, and he smiled as he called out, "You have no idea how silly the two of you looked. Jane, I wouldn't have believed it if I hadn't seen the sight myself. And you even started this fracas."

Jane stared at him as her mouth dropped open, leaving a slit between her lips. He must have been spying on them from behind the trees, for she surely would have noticed him if he had been standing near the water. And he had been there from the beginning of their little battle. Had he seen her enter the water? Why, she'd hiked her skirts clear up to her. . . Colorless heat suffused her face and branched out to her ears.

"Luke Reiley!" Jane jammed her fists onto her hips. "You were spying on us. Just how long did you hide behind those trees watching us?"

Luke waded over to the girls, a telling blush creeping up his neck. "I wasn't spying exactly. . . ." A sheepish grin and hands that were turned palms-up completed his sentence.

Jane looked at Elizabeth and saw a mischievous glint in her eyes. Jane hadn't known Elizabeth very long, but she was certainly capable of reading the intent in her eyes. Jane's eyes took on an impish look of their own before both of them reached into the creek and showered Luke with simultaneous sprays of water.

"Hey!" Luke shouted with surprise as he put his hands out to ward off the gush of water.

Jane and Elizabeth advanced on him, getting bolder as he retreated from them. Elizabeth was giggling with delight, and Jane herself was having a good laugh at Luke's expense when he suddenly lost his footing and toppled backward into the bubbling brook.

He landed with a splash, and Jane and Elizabeth stopped their hands in midair. Luke looked momentarily shocked, as if he weren't sure how he came to be sitting in the middle of the creek.

"Luke! Are you all right?" It was Elizabeth who recovered first.

Luke shook his head to clear it, sending droplets of water everywhere. "I'm fine, I think. My foot slipped on a rock," he said, making no effort to stand. "Well, what are you waiting for? The least the two of you could do is help me up."

Jane and Elizabeth each extended a hand to Luke. Jane no sooner felt her hand being engulfed by his than she felt a powerful tug that sent her plunging into the water beside Luke. She automatically flung her other hand out to break her fall but, even so, she found herself sitting in the creek only inches from Luke. Elizabeth came splashing in only a second behind her. Luke's laughter followed shortly after.

Elizabeth wiped the droplets from her face. "I can't believe you did that! We're soaking wet!"

Luke seemed hardly able to contain himself. "You were already wet anyway."

He turned to look at Jane just then, and she was momentarily stunned by the beautiful expression on his face. His eyes were a reflection of the water that surrounded them, twinkling as the sun played with its surface. Crinkles lined his eyes, and his one dimple appeared to the left of his smiling mouth, inducing Jane's smile. If a man could be described as beautiful, Luke was surely such a man. Jane memorized his expression, intending to sketch him later.

Elizabeth stood to her feet with a swash, drawing Luke's attention once again. Within moments, another water war commenced, and the three frolicked audaciously in the creek.

Later that afternoon, as she and Elizabeth walked back to the house, their dresses clinging stubbornly to their legs, Jane realized she could not recall having ever enjoyed herself more.

∿

The heat in the cottage was so stifling that evening that Jane opened the front and back doors to draw in the cooler evening air. Her mission that night had been to sketch Luke and, since the cabin's heat was unbearable, she took her tools out to the front porch. After propping up her tablet, Jane closed her eyes for a moment to recall the details of his face. She saw clearly in her mind's eye the expression he'd worn that afternoon. Eager to begin, Jane picked up her lead pencil and began sketching the outline of his face. She would put the sky in the background, she decided as her pencil flew in familiar form around the page. Perhaps some wispy clouds, but nothing so detailed as to pull one's attention from his face.

Once the outline of his face was complete, Jane executed the feathery strokes that would represent Luke's hair, leaving the areas white that would become highlights. His wavy brown hair seemed to attract the sunlight, just as his eyes did. Of course, one could see highlights on dark eyes and hair much easier than on light. Jane wondered if her own eyes reflected the sun. They were very dark, after all.

Luke's eyes were even easier to portray than his hair— eyes, forever laughing and flickering, giving off warm, vibrant light.

With her pencil, she gently darkened in the hollows of his face and the dimple that adorned his left cheek. The shadowing and highlighting gradually gave birth to Luke's familiar face. This was the part Jane liked most about drawing: the fine details that perfected the representation. Jane worked diligently on each feature, leaving the mouth for last, since she couldn't remember exactly the shape of his lips.

When the sun sank in the sky, withdrawing the last of the day's light, Jane stretched her taut neck and shoulder muscles. She'd been sitting motionless for well over an hour. Her work had paid off though, for staring up at her from the tablet was Luke. At least, Luke without his mouth. She would have to take particular notice of his lips tomorrow.

As she studied her handiwork, Jane realized for the first time that she no longer found Luke an annoyance. In fact, she had to admit, she was growing to like him. A smile formed of its own volition. Yes, perhaps Luke wasn't so bad after all.

nine

Getting breakfast on the table the next morning was a hassle. Elizabeth overslept, then scurried to gather the eggs while Jane rushed to have the food ready before Luke returned from his morning chores. Everything that could have gone wrong did: the bacon burned, the water boiled over, and in her hurry, she sloshed milk all over her frock.

Even so, she managed to have the food ready by the time Luke had washed up. The acrid smell of smoke had dissipated somewhat, and most of the bacon had been salvageable. Elizabeth scooted into her seat just as Jane placed the milk pitcher on the table.

Luke and Elizabeth carried the conversation throughout the meal, while Jane mentally reviewed the tasks she needed to do by day's end.

When Elizabeth finished eating, she excused herself from the table. "I'll do the dishes, Jane. You had to fix breakfast all by yourself, and it was my fault for sleeping late."

Jane thanked her as she passed her with an armful of dishes. Luke leaned toward her, helping himself to another piece of bacon when Jane suddenly remembered her intent to study the shape of his lips. She lowered her fork and focused on Luke's mouth, narrowing her eyes and unconsciously biting her own lip in concentration. His lower lip was average sized, but his upper lip was rather full for a man's, she thought. She wondered if it thinned much when he smiled. She would have to find out, since he was smiling in his portrait. If only he would smile so she could see. . .

Jane felt a prickling heat that crawled up her arms and converged at the base of her neck before suffusing her face. She knew without looking she'd been caught. Slowly, with instinctive dread, she raised her eyes to meet his.

His dark brows knotted in confusion, and she opened her mouth to explain. Just as quickly, she snapped it shut. What was she going to say—that she was studying his features so she could complete his portrait? What would he think of that? She felt warmth flood her face and was glad the heat would not culminate in a telltale blush.

Luke's eyes darted down to her mouth. She stilled, afraid to blink or even swallow. The moment dragged on, a tense silence enshrouding them.

Suddenly, Luke cleared his throat, shattering the silence and breaking the trance. Both of them awkwardly turned their attention to their plates as Elizabeth returned to retrieve more dishes.

It was unlike Luke to be so quiet and reflective. Why hadn't he made a joke or asked if he had preserves on his chin, anything but sit there all tongue-tied. And what must he think of her—staring at his lips from across the table like a brazen wench. Jane excused herself, her head bent in mortification as she carried her dishes to the basin in trembling hands that threatened to reduce the china to a stack of shards.

Elizabeth waved off her offer of help, so Jane thankfully made an excuse and retreated to her cottage. She desperately needed to compose herself. She'd have to face him eventually. Yet, perhaps, by tonight he would have forgotten her behavior.

Jane plopped onto the sofa and covered her face with shaking hands. *What a ninny I am! He probably thinks I'm besotted with him! What else could he think?*

Oh, why hadn't she just admitted to the sketch? She should have realized the conclusion he would draw from her overt gawking! Well, she couldn't admit to the sketch now. That, combined with this morning's behavior, would certainly lead him to the wrong conclusion.

Jane let her head drop back against the sofa and released a puff of breath. This wasn't like her at all—brooding over Luke's interpretations of her feelings. Why, she had never had any trouble at all telling Luke exactly what she thought! In fact, it had always seemed beyond her to edit her words where he was concerned.

Why was this occasion so different? Why hadn't she just blurted out her feelings as she usually did instead of making him think she was enamored with him? Could there be a bit of truth in there somewhere?

❧

The afternoon flowed by like a swelling river. Chores consumed every moment and, although Elizabeth offered her help, Jane refused. The little girl had been forced to grow up too quickly and deserved some playtime while she was still a youngster.

Jane's mind was as active as her hands. She couldn't help but replay this morning's breakfast incident repeatedly. Luke had seemed almost as mesmerized as Jane had felt. She mentally scolded herself. If he seemed a bit struck, it was only because she'd shocked him. Looking at it from

Luke's point of view, she realized he must be confused. After all, Jane had never hid her annoyance with him. In fact, she'd been inexcusably obvious.

And now, she'd given Luke reason to believe she was attracted to him. Her stomach fluttered. What if it was true? She quickly dismissed the idea, uncomfortable with giving the matter even a moment's consideration. Still, she was aware that something was happening within her.

On Saturday morning, Luke asked Jane if she'd like to have another riding lesson that night. Anxious, but not about to show it, Jane consented.

In the afternoon, she and Elizabeth took the wagon to town for supplies. While they were in the store, Jane spotted Elizabeth admiring a bolt of fabric in a lovely buttercup yellow. Spontaneously, Jane purchased enough of the material to make Elizabeth a new gown and watched Elizabeth hop up and down with excitement. Judging by the girl's snug clothes, it had been a while since she'd worn a new dress. When they left the store, lengths of ribbons and lace were also tucked away in the brown wrapping paper.

Later, Jane measured Elizabeth and showed her how to start a garment. Before they realized, the supper hour approached, and they scurried through the preparations.

After the meal, Luke told her he'd saddle Brownie and wait for her by the stable. She informed him she would need to change her dress. After he left, Elizabeth addressed Jane with her eyes alight. "Can I watch this time? Please?"

Jane bit her lip. She was not ready for an audience yet, but how could she refuse? Then she had an idea. "Actually, I was thinking you might like to work on your dress."

"Oh, can I?" she asked with wide eyes. "All by myself?"

"You can start basting it, and tomorrow I'll check and see how you did."

Jane helped Elizabeth begin the task, then rushed to the cottage, where she selected a serviceable dress of brown muslin. A quick glance in the mirror told her several wisps of hair had escaped their knot, but she had already kept Luke waiting too long, so she hurried out the door.

Luke was waiting by the stables as promised, his strong hands stroking Brownie's taut neck. Beside him stood a mammoth black horse with a beautiful shiny coat, saddled and ready to go. Luke gave Brownie a final pat before turning to acknowledge Jane. "I was beginning to think you were going to stand me up."

"I had to help Elizabeth with some sewing," she said, staring anxiously at the second horse.

Luke must have noticed her hesitancy. "This is Ebony. I thought maybe you'd like to have Brownie to yourself this time."

"Well. . ."

"You'll be fine. I can ride right beside you. We'll just walk the horses across the field, nice and slow."

"I suppose I can give it a try." At least she wouldn't have Luke's disconcerting presence behind her.

Luke boosted her onto the horse, and Jane settled on the creaking saddle. After releasing the saddle horn and taking the reins, she felt quite comfortable atop the horse. She was not nearly as afraid of falling off as she was last time. A small, proud smile formed unconsciously on her lips as she waited for Luke to mount Ebony.

With a nudge of their heels, the horses meandered beyond

the stables and into the high prairie grass. The unevenness of the packed ground made for a bumpy ride and, as Brownie treaded over it, Jane held herself rigid for fear of falling off.

"Loosen up, Jane. Let your body move with the horse's."

Jane did as he said and soon realized that giving in to the motion was easier than fighting against it.

"You're doing well."

They traveled for a spell in comfortable silence, enjoying the beautiful sunset. Jane paid particular attention to the swatches of pink and orange, noting the way the colors faded into the sky above them. The sun was a fiery globe sinking into the ground like butter melting in a frying pan. She longed to attempt the impossible challenge of capturing this brilliant light with paint.

Luke interrupted her reverie. "I've been meaning to tell you how much I appreciate all you've done with Elizabeth —the sewing and such. Mama taught her the basics, but she really did need to start learning some practical things."

"Why, I haven't minded at all. But, I must warn you, I'm not much of a seamstress. Cassy, though, she's. . ." Jane stopped abruptly and bit her lip. She kept her eyes straight ahead and hoped that somehow Luke hadn't heard her last words. An awkward silence hovered around them.

"Jane. . .you don't have to avoid the subject of your sister. She is, after all, going to be home in two weeks."

"I just didn't want to—"

"It's okay. Now, what were you going to say?"

"I was just going to say Cassy's the seamstress in our family. She made her wedding gown, you know."

"No, I didn't. That'd be a pretty handy talent to have—especially here in Cedar Springs."

Jane knew he was referring to the selection the town store carried—pitifully small compared to the infinite choices available in the stores of Philadelphia. Of course, you could hardly compare the two places. All things considered, Jane thought she preferred the tranquility of Cedar Springs to the bustling city of Philadelphia. The people seemed friendlier here.

"You've gotten mighty quiet all of a sudden."

"I was just thinking how much I like living here. I was anxious about coming at first, but now that I'm here, I find I don't want to leave."

Luke paused so long that Jane glanced his way. "What?" she asked.

Luke squirmed in his saddle and opened his mouth twice before he finally uttered a word. "You've been mighty kind to help us out here, Jane. But. . .you do realize when Caleb and Cassy come back, Cassy will, you know, take over the house and all. . . ."

Jane stared at Luke, confused. Why in the world was he talking about. . .? Her mind's wheels skidded to an abrupt halt before churning away again at twice their normal pace. *He must've thought I meant living here on his property. Surely he didn't think I was dropping a hint—hoping he'd allow me to stay after Cassy and Caleb come back.* Jane observed Luke in the thick silence. He was rubbing his jaw in a restless manner and a telling red flush had crept up his neck.

Jane hurried to set things straight. "I didn't mean I like it *here,* at your house. I meant I liked it in Cedar Springs—

that I didn't want to return to Philadelphia."

Luke sat up straight, and his mouth slowly formed into a familiar smile before giving way to laughter. "Oh! I thought you meant—"

"I know what you thought. But, although I've enjoyed my time here, I'm quite content to go back to my family. They'll need my help at the restaurant. We should be open for business when Cassy and Caleb return, you know."

"Yes, I've noticed the construction progress. From the look of things, your parents' house is sizable."

Jane paused while Brownie plodded across a narrow trickling stream. "This one will surely be the largest house we've ever lived in. Mama said mine and Katy's room is going to be as big as the entire upstairs of our rental. Why, once Katy is married off, I'll have all that space to myself."

Jane turned with a smile to meet Luke's gaze. Instead of his usual lopsided grin, she found his mouth to be drawn in a straight line and his eyebrows pulled together in confusion. *What have I said now?* she thought, as she turned forward. They rode in silence for a few moments.

"What about you, Jane? Aren't you planning to marry?"

The words pierced a vulnerable spot in her heart, inducing an almost physical pain. How could he even ask? Couldn't he see no man alive would want her? Her—with her spindly frame and homely face?

Jane didn't realize her eyes were brimming with tears until they completely obscured her vision. She turned her face away from Luke, relieved he was riding slightly behind her, and rapidly blinked away the tears. She had hardly composed herself when he nudged his mount to her side.

"Did I say something wrong?" His words were soft once

again, but Jane clenched her teeth together, hardening her jaw line.

"I'm sorry if I spoke out of turn."

Jane knew the moment Luke's gaze turned away, and she relaxed once again. Didn't he realize she wasn't like other women? The fact certainly seemed obvious to everyone else. Even her childhood schoolmates understood that marriage was a futile pursuit for someone like Jane. They'd drilled as much into her head repeatedly with their taunts and cruelty.

No one would ever want her. Not for a wife.

Jane was so absorbed in her thoughts she didn't notice that Luke had turned his horse toward home and that Brownie had followed. It was just as well. Her back was beginning to ache, and the hard saddle was inflicting a pain of its own kind.

Uneasy silence prevailed for the duration of the ride. Jane was not inclined to break it, and Luke also seemed reluctant to engage in casual conversation. Jane concentrated instead on the sounds around her. The whisper of the prairie grasses as they swished through them. The hooting of a distant owl. The rustling of the wind moving through the trees. Darkness enveloped them, exchanging the vibrant colors of day with the flat, monochromatic colors of night. When they neared the stable, she arched her back with relief, anticipating the end of the ride.

They reached the stable doors, and Luke dismounted, then rounded Jane's horse to assist her. She was almost ready to dismount on her own, but the distance between the stirrups and the ground made her hesitate.

Without words, Luke reached out and placed his hands

on Jane's waist as she slid her leg around Brownie's backside. Her right foot quickly found the ground, then she worked her left foot out of the stirrup—a feat that was easier said than done, given that the stirrup was nearly waist-high. She heard Luke chuckle, his breath stirring the wisps of hair near her ear. Once she'd extracted her foot, Jane breathed a laugh and turned to meet his gaze.

His eyes were laughing, though not at her this time, but with her. They seemed to darken in the dusky light, and Jane wondered if it was an illusion. His dimple disappeared as the smile slid quietly from his face, and the laugh lines around his eyes smoothed out to match the tanned planes of his face.

ten

Jane's heart thudded in her chest. Suddenly she became very aware of his strong hands encompassing her waist. Time seemed to stop.

The moment was nothing and everything all at once. No movement, no words. Just a silent meeting of two souls. Their breaths mingled, and Jane felt the warmth of his body. His eyes shifted to her lips, and Jane parted them in wonder. For one anxious moment, Jane thought he meant to kiss her, and she unconsciously wetted her lips.

The movement broke the spell. Luke cleared his throat, then removed his hands and stepped away, leaving Jane feeling strangely bereft. He rubbed the back of his neck and muttered something unintelligible before proceeding to unsaddle his horse. Jane retreated to her cottage as fast as her legs would carry her.

Once she was safely inside, she leaned against the door and drew a deep, shuddering breath. What had happened back there? She knew she was inexperienced in matters of the heart, but surely she hadn't mistaken the look in his eyes. The tender heat in his look had doubled her heart rate.

But what about Cassy? Could he be losing his feelings for her and acquiring feelings for Jane? Surely not. A man who was besotted with her beautiful sister could never be attracted to her.

Yet, there had been no mistaking the look in his eyes.

Even good friends did not stare at one another in such a fashion. And his hands. . .he had left them resting heavily on her waist. Jane lifted a trembling hand to her still-racing heart.

There was no mistaking her own reactions either. Perhaps, she had denied her feelings before, but now she was forced to face the truth. She had enjoyed his closeness and craved the elusive kiss. She didn't know how it had happened. Heaven knew she used to think of Luke as a thorn in her side.

Pushing herself away from the door, she considered finishing Luke's portrait, but instead succumbed to her sudden weariness and retired for the night. Tomorrow she'd spend time with her family and enjoy a vital reprieve from him.

೫

Luke propped his bare feet up on the footstool and stared silently into the fireplace's cold grate. He still wasn't used to having all this time to himself in the evening after Elizabeth went to bed. He and Caleb used to discuss ranch matters or even personal matters during this time. Now he was on his own.

Perhaps all this extra quiet time had contributed to his confusion. After all, he certainly had more time to dwell on his feelings and such. Still, he couldn't help but wonder what was going on with his feelings for Jane. Moments ago he had been mesmerized by her eyes, his hands resting on the gentle curve of her hips, feeling all the things a man feels toward a woman he's attracted to. Her eyes had been alive with laughter as she'd turned to look at him, then the laughter had faded to a tender, captivating vulnerability. She'd looked so confused and, when her lips had parted, he'd been tempted to taste them with his own. He'd come so close, in fact, that he now wondered how he'd been able to stop himself.

But he was so bewildered about his own feelings and didn't want to trifle with Jane's affections. Luke chuckled to himself. Who was he kidding? Jane would have probably walloped him upside the head if he'd attempted to kiss her. She'd made no secret of her feelings toward him.

But what was going on within him? What of his feelings for Cassy? He'd never been a fickle person. Surely he couldn't have fallen out of love with Cassy so soon. When she came back, the old feelings would likely resurface, and he would find himself soaking in the same pickle barrel. But what if his feelings for Cassy had been shallow? What if the feelings he was having for Jane were the real thing? Surely it wouldn't hurt to follow them a little—give them a chance to grow and develop.

&

The next morning, Jane dressed with care, selecting her most becoming dress, an ivory gown adorned with lace around the neck and sleeves. After pressing out the creases, she slipped into the dress and quickly arranged her hair. She didn't ask herself why she was taking pains with her appearance, but on a deeper level, she knew the effort had something to do with Luke.

Before heading out the door, she pinched her cheeks, producing a rosy glow, and admitted for once she felt almost satisfied with her appearance.

Jane and Elizabeth prepared breakfast with practiced ease and, just as they placed the last platter on the table, Luke entered the house.

"Good morning."

Elizabeth responded in kind, and Jane mumbled a "good morning" of her own. As they seated themselves, Jane felt Luke's perusal, and her heart tapped at a speedy tempo. She would not look at him. She would not.

Jane raised her eyes to meet Luke's gaze. He wore a merry grin, and his twinkling eyes revealed his good mood. "You look especially lovely this morning."

Jane's lashes fell. "Thank you."

"Well, how about me?" Elizabeth pouted, barely suppressing her smile, in a way that was little girl and grown woman all rolled into one.

"Ah. . ." Luke examined her appearance through pretend spectacles. "Yes, Miss Reiley, you do look rather fetching this morning," he said with mock gravity. "Especially with that dab of gravy on your chin."

Elizabeth touched her chin and drew her hand away to find that he'd been telling the truth. Jane joined in the resulting laughter.

With the tension broken, Jane relaxed enough to enjoy breakfast. Sundays were always rushed with the effort of morning chores, but soon they were on their way to church. Elizabeth chattered about her friend Mary and the fort they were planning to build—for girls only—she added with emphasis. Jane and Luke shared smiles of mature understanding, knowing in a couple years Elizabeth's opinion of boys would change.

The day was already warm, but the gusts of wind held the heat at bay. As she watched Elizabeth attempt to restrain her flying tresses, Jane was glad her hair was neatly scraped back in a roll at her neck. She glanced sideways and watched as the wind toyed with Luke's hair, tossing a lock rebelliously in his eyes. She wondered if his hair was as soft as it looked.

When they arrived in the churchyard, Luke went to talk to the pianist about the songs he'd chosen, and Jane seated herself beside Elizabeth, not wanting to leave her alone. Soon, her family arrived, and Jane greeted each of them. She'd missed her family these past two weeks and was glad she would be spending the day with them.

Sara and Nathan McClain arrived with their newborn and were instantly swarmed by women and children alike. Elizabeth wanted to join the throng, but Jane thought it best to wait until after the service since they'd already seen the baby.

Everyone found a seat when the pianist began playing, then Luke went forward to lead the singing. His rich, baritone voice carried throughout the small building, blending with the tones of soprano and bass.

They were well into the second verse when the door to the rear of the building opened, bringing in a warm gust of wind. A young woman entered, and Jane recognized her as the beautiful woman she'd seen at church once before. Rather than slipping into a back pew, she sashayed up to the third row. Jane couldn't help but notice the young men's heads turning as she walked by. A twinge of jealousy pricked Jane. How nice it must be to have that effect on people.

When the singing ended, Luke seated himself on the other side of Elizabeth, and the Reverend Hill stepped forward. He opened with a joke, as he seemed to be in the habit of doing, and the congregation chuckled in response.

Once he started his sermon, Jane let her mind wander.

She thought about Sara and her little baby and smiled along with everyone else when the newborn emitted a tiny squeak. Next, her attention shifted to the young lady in the third row. *I wonder who she is,* Jane thought. Her flaxen hair was pulled up into a loose knot, and the ends dangled in contrived ringlets past her shoulders. She was beautiful, there was no doubt of that, but she was a different kind of beautiful than her sisters. Cassy and Katy were intrinsic beauties, like their mother. Their blond good looks were natural—flawless skin, silky hair, and striking eyes. This young woman had nice attributes, but they were enhanced by artificial means. It was obvious she wore color on her face, and Jane was sure the last time she'd seen the woman, her hair had been straight as a pin.

Jane wondered which look men preferred. She supposed that depended upon the man. Certainly Caleb must have preferred her sister's natural beauty, but her earlier observations confirmed the fact that other men appreciated this woman's efforts.

By the end of the service, Jane was weary of sitting and glad to stand and stretch her legs. Luke and Elizabeth said their good-byes and made their way toward the back of the church as Jane stooped to retrieve her handbag. When she stood, she noticed the young woman withdrawing from a group of men and was startled to see the newcomer moving toward her. The woman stepped daintily around other people on her way, her eyes fixed upon Jane.

As she neared, Jane noted the exquisite detail of her dress. It was ivory, as was Jane's, but that's where the similarities ended. The woman's fitted bodice called attention to her curvy figure, and the daring neckline stopped just short of indecent. The full skirts swished with her every step, jostling the ruffles at the hem. Her petite frame made her seem doll-like and, as she approached, Jane slumped in an effort to hide her gangliness.

"Good day." The woman offered a limp hand and a cool smile. "I don't believe we've met."

Jane extended her own hand and returned the woman's smile. "Hello, I'm Jane."

"Mara Lawton. My family owns the carriage works business at the edge of town." Mara withdrew her hand and tilted her chin a bit higher. Jane had the feeling she was about to say something else, but just then Katy approached. "Mama wants to know if you'll be coming for dinner, Jane."

Jane turned her attention to her sister. "Oh. . .yes, I'll be there in a moment."

Katy offered Mara a smile, and Mara offered a distracted one of her own.

Mara's mouth had dropped open, and her eyes held a hint of disbelief as they shifted from Jane to Katy, then back to Jane again. There was something in that look that made her wary.

"Why, I can't believe. . . You can't be. . ."

Jane bit her lip, her gaze darting around the room in search of an escape. Heat curdled her stomach, and her heart's tempo accelerated.

"Why, you're not one of the Coopers', are you?" Mara exclaimed, her skepticism changing into something heartless, cruel.

"Yes, I am." Jane forced the words and, to her relief,

they came out sounding confident. Her mouth had grown dry in contrast to her sweaty palms, which she dried by smoothing down the folds in her skirt.

Mara's mouth curled up in a simulated smile, and she placed a manicured hand to her chest in surprise. "I can hardly believe it! You don't resemble them at all."

Jane cringed and wished desperately Mara would lower her voice. Several people were looking their way, including Luke, and her humiliation multiplied a hundredfold. She desperately scanned the room for her family and realized, to her dismay, they were nowhere to be seen.

Escape came in an unlikely form. A handsome young man approached and waited until he drew Mara's attention. He would have been hard to overlook with his golden good looks and startling blue eyes, but Mara managed to do just that for a long moment. She finally acknowledged his presence by tilting her head coquettishly to meet his eyes and planting a coy smile upon her lips.

Jane sagged in relief to have the attention diverted. All that was in her urged her to flee, but a lifetime of good etiquette held her motionless. She listened to the husky voice of the young man.

"You haven't given me your answer yet, Mara, about the picnic." For all his manly height and appearance, his voice quivered in hope.

"Hmm, I suppose I haven't, have I?" She fluttered her lashes in an obvious display of flirtation and tapped a long fingernail against her cherry lips. "Could I possibly have another day to consider, Joshua? I'm afraid I've not had a spare moment to consider your offer."

The young man relaxed a bit and allowed a heartened

smile. "Sure, that'd be fine. May I escort you home?" he asked, offering her his arm.

Mara paused just long enough to make Joshua squirm. "I suppose that would be all right." She delicately linked her arm with his, then turned suddenly as if just remembering Jane's presence. "Oh. Good day, uh. . ." She arched her brows and left the sentence dangling for Jane to finish.

"Jane." She lowered her eyes.

"Yes, of course," she said offhandedly as she waltzed away on the arm of the man.

Jane rummaged through her handbag as if searching for something. Anything to stall for time. She did not want another confrontation with Mara.

Her hands trembled pitifully, and she was glad there was no one around to witness her anxiety. Everyone was moving toward the door and filing out of the building after shaking hands with the Reverend Hill. Finally, Jane gathered her belongings and joined the end of the line. She moved mechanically, her mind barely registering her encounter with the minister.

Once out the door, she saw her family waiting in the wagon and proceeded toward them. She thanked them for waiting, but said she'd prefer to walk the short distance to their home. The wagon clattered away, and Jane began walking, her numb mind instructing her limbs to move. She was oblivious to the other people standing around the churchyard. Oblivious to the wind that tugged on her skirts. Slowly the numbness wore away, leaving an aching emptiness within her.

How could she have thought, even for a moment, that Luke might be interested in her? She gave a harsh laugh.

How foolish she had been! He was not attracted to her. No one would ever be attracted to her. If anything, it was pity Luke felt for her. Pity that she was born ugly, with no hope of ever securing a husband. That she'd had the audacity to think Luke might grow to love her made her cringe with bitterness.

The town's buildings swam before her eyes, but she gritted her teeth and forbade herself to let a single tear fall. This was her own fault. She'd known all along what her place was. She had let herself forget—had foolishly allowed herself to wallow in her own impossible dreams. *Let this be a lesson. The next time Luke shows me kindness, I will remember it's pity alone.*

She thought of Mara's cruel words and felt the pit of her stomach go hot all over again. The woman had enjoyed her discomfort, relished it even, and would have probably taken the humiliation further if she hadn't been interrupted by that poor young man. Was that the sort of woman a man liked? Were men really willing to tolerate a heartless, conniving woman as long as she was pretty to look at?

The thought disgusted her. Life was so unfair.

Why should someone like herself have to suffer with a homely appearance, while someone like Mara, with an evil heart, was blessed with the face of an angel. What sense did that make? The question was posed to no one in particular, but her heart silently addressed God.

Jane walked, unseeing, past the new restaurant. In fact, she was surprised when she came upon the Coopes' rental house. Knowing she must collect herself, she breathed a deep sigh and tried to relax the taut, frowning muscles of her face. Her mother was incredibly intuitive about her children's feelings, and Jane didn't want to talk about her encounter with Mara, nor her own feelings.

As Jane turned the rusty doorknob and entered the house, the sweet smell of baked ham assaulted her senses.

"Is that you, Jane?" called her mother from the kitchen.

"Yes, Mother."

"Can you wash up and give me a hand?"

Jane strode past her mother and Katy to the kitchen basin and pumped water.

"It was a thoughtful sermon, wasn't it?" Her mother stirred the beans and added a pinch of salt.

Jane gave a noncommittal grunt, leaving Katy to comment on the service in detail. Mostly who was wearing what and who was courting whom. She giggled girlishly as she placed the dishes on the table and told Jane and her mother the joke her friend Nancy had shared that morning. Her mother laughed in response.

After dinner, the family scattered in different directions. Katy took David to see the spring after which the town was named. They had asked Jane to accompany them, but she was not in the mood for conversation. Her father had gone into the parlor to read and, judging by the odorous puffs of thick haze rising above his head, to smoke his pipe. Jane intended to retreat to her room and perhaps draw a bit once she finished washing the dinner dishes.

Her mother returned from the table with an empty platter and clanked it down on the counter. "Something wrong, sweetheart?" Mrs. Cooper paused a moment, and Jane felt her examination.

"No, Mama. I'm fine."

Her mother went back to the table for more dishes. "I

saw you talking to that Lawton girl. Did she say something to upset you?"

Jane paused for the briefest of moments, then opened her mouth to deny it. Her mother spoke first.

"A mother can always tell, you know. You'll see what I mean when you have children of your own. It's like they're a part of you somehow, and you can tell when they're hurting. Sometimes you wish you could feel their pain for them." Another dish clanked onto the pile.

Jane's lips tightened when her mother mentioned having children. Who was she kidding? Jane pulled the next dish into the basin and began scrubbing it vigorously. Surely her own mother knew she would never succeed in interesting any man. Jane, who had never even had a beau. She clenched her jaw as her mother continued.

"But that's not the way God made us. We each have to endure our own pain, and I suppose that's best. But it's hard watching your own children struggle and not being able to help." Mrs. Cooper turned from the table with a smile. "You'll see what I mean one day."

Jane dropped the pot she was washing with a plop. "No. I won't." The words were sharp and part of her wished she could take them back. She was afraid to look at her mother, but saw from her peripheral vision that she had frozen in place.

"What do you mean?" The soft-spoken words should have gentled her spirit, but instead they ignited the spark that had been burning within her all morning—indeed, all her life.

"Don't you understand, Mother?" Jane had ceased her washing, but her hands remained in the water, curled into fists, and her eyes were focused unseeingly on a tree out-side the window. "I'm never going to have children. I'm never going to marry." She laughed harshly. "What man would ever want me?"

She turned quickly and met her mother's stricken stare. "Can you answer me that, Mama? What man is ever going to want a skinny, ugly wife?"

Jane turned back to the basin and began vigorously washing the dishes again, trying to wipe her mother's hurt look from her memory. "What man is ever going to want me when they can have someone beautiful and dainty, like Cassy, or Katy, or even Mara?"

The room swelled with silence until Jane wished she'd kept her mouth shut. Only the splashing of dishwater could be heard until the clicking of her mother's heels on the plank floor joined in to create a pathetic-sounding symphony.

Mrs. Cooper stopped beside Jane and laid a hand on her arm to halt Jane's movements. Jane ceased her task, but refrained from looking into her mother's eyes, which, she knew, would reflect the hurt she had seen in her gaze moments ago.

"You are special, Jane," her mother said softly. "God made you just the way you are, and I am glad." Jane turned to meet her mother's stare, angered that her mother would say such a thing, yet having too much respect to blurt out her bitter feelings. Her mother read her face. "You are not ugly or gawky, and you mustn't compare yourself to others." Her mother touched Jane's chin and turned her head toward her once again. "There is nothing wrong with the way you are. You are beautiful in your own way, and one day some man is going to see you for the way you are: beautiful inside *and* out."

Jane bit the inside of her lip to prevent more words from spewing out. It would do no good. Every mother thought their child was something special, and nothing she could say would convince her otherwise.

Jane heard her mother sigh softly before turning to retrieve more dishes. She was relieved the conversation was over. Her mother meant well, but she was mistaken. What would her mother know of being ugly? She'd been born a beauty herself and, to hear her father tell it, every young man in Philadelphia had vied for her attention. No, her mother didn't know what it was like.

Jane rushed through the dishes, then dumped the water out the back door. When she returned, she was relieved to see her mother was gone, and she took the opportunity to escape to the solitude of her room.

Once there, Jane began a sketch of the mountains off in the distance, but her mind was not on the project, and her attempts were futile. She stood back and inspected her work. Pitiful. She'd been doing nicer work when she was thirteen. She took the sketch and wadded it up in a ball, then flung it in the trash. Her mood today was not conducive to creativity. Instead, she felt more like crawling into a cave and staying there until Cassy and Caleb came back.

Oh, how she wished she didn't have to return to the Reileys' place! She had made a fool of herself by assuming Luke's interest in her indicated attraction. She cringed at the memory of the night before, then threw herself on the bed and pulled the quilt over her head, trying to smother the memory from her mind. If only it were that easy.

Surely Luke must have read the attraction in her face the night before and realized she had wanted his kiss. Oh, the mortification! She couldn't bear such a humiliation. How he must pity her: *Poor Jane. No one will ever want her.*

A rare tear slid from beneath her closed eyelids, and she swept it away brusquely with the corner of her quilt. She would not make a fool of herself again. She wasn't sure why she'd let her defenses down where Luke was concerned, but they would go right back up. She would put the distance back in their relationship, and she would allow him to pity her no more.

eleven

When Jane opened her eyes the next morning, the faint light of dawn was seeping through her window sheers. Time to get up. With a groan of protest, she pulled the cover over her head. She dreaded facing Luke this morning.

The previous night, she'd had her father bring her over just before twilight and, just as she'd hoped, she'd managed to dart into her cottage, deftly avoiding Luke.

Jane heaved a sigh and kicked off the light blanket. There would be no avoiding Luke today. She scurried around getting ready, aware the sun was over the horizon, and Luke would be expecting breakfast on the table.

When she entered Luke's house, she found Elizabeth in the kitchen cracking fresh eggs into a skillet.

"Sorry I'm late. Thanks for starting breakfast."

Elizabeth smiled sweetly. "That's okay. There's no rush this morning anyway. Luke got an early start and has already headed out."

Part of Jane felt like shouting for joy, but another part—a part she quickly suppressed—felt a twinge of disappointment. She wondered if she was losing her heart to Luke. What a disaster that would be; loving a man who was in love with her sister and who felt only pity for her.

Jane's mind wandered throughout the meal, while Elizabeth chattered about her friends. She mustn't let her feelings for Luke grow beyond what they were already.

How had this happened? She remembered with clarity how she'd felt about Luke in the beginning. Why, he had exasperated her like an older brother. Worse even. He'd had the unique ability to say just the thing to send her flying into a fit of rage.

Yet he hadn't changed, really. He still taunted her in the same way. No, she was the one who had changed. Somehow she'd grown used to his teasing, even become fond of it. He had sanded away her layer of hostility, exposing the vulnerable surface beneath.

She resigned herself to avoiding Luke. That was the only way to prevent her increasing attachment to him. Just two weeks remained before Cassy and Caleb returned. She would just spend as little time as possible around Luke and remain detached when he was near. No more horseback riding lessons, for certain. Anyway, she felt she was able to do—

Jane abruptly noticed the silence and darted a look at Elizabeth, who was staring at her with a cocked eyebrow and an amused smile.

"Did you say something?" Jane asked sheepishly.

Elizabeth laughed. "You haven't heard anything I've said, have you?"

Jane smiled sheepishly. What a dreadful example she set for this young girl, letting her mind drift away while she talked. "I'm sorry, Elizabeth."

With a chuckle, Elizabeth forgave her and started on a new subject.

Later that afternoon, Jane yanked the last handful of weeds from the vegetable garden, stood to her feet, and placed a hand on her aching back. She noted the position of the sun in the sky and realized she had at least an hour before she had to start supper, so she determined to weed the flowerbed at the front of the house. This was the one task she'd neglected since she'd been here and, as she approached the garden, she saw to her dismay that the weeds had taken over the ground, spreading like a disease across the colorful pallet.

With a resigned sigh, Jane lowered herself to her knees and began ruthlessly snatching clusters of stubborn weeds. Now that she saw the work before her, she wished she had not sent Elizabeth to Mary's house to play.

She wasn't sure how long she'd been toiling when a shadow fell across the flowerbed. Gasping in surprise, she turned and saw Luke's silhouette, her heart suddenly hammering.

"You might at least give me a warning before you sneak up on me like that!" Her sharp words reflected her irritation and dimmed the smile in his eyes.

"Sorry. Didn't mean to scare you."

Jane returned to her work, more to occupy her hands than anything. Perhaps he would sense her withdrawal and go away. Her head told her this was what she wanted, but her heart thumped tenaciously, as if to refute her thoughts.

Luke's boots shuffled beside her, stirring up puffs of dirt. His perusal made her uneasy. "I hope you don't think we're going to eat early, because I haven't even started supper yet," she spat.

Luke flinched at her biting tone. "No. . . I was just going to go wash up in the creek. I'll be back around suppertime."

Jane heard the confusion and hurt in his voice and felt a

pang of guilt. Despite herself, she felt the need to smooth things over a bit. "I'm almost finished here, then I'll start supper."

Luke was already backing away and shoving his hat on his head. "No hurry." Ducking his head, he turned and ambled toward the creek.

Jane watched his back as he walked away. His shoulders slumped, and once again Jane felt the stab of guilt. She'd hurt his feelings. She was sorry that things had to be this way, but she knew of no other course of action to keep a distance between them. When Luke turned back to look at her, she quickly pretended to be absorbed in her work.

❧

Supper that night was a quiet affair. Even Elizabeth seemed caught up in her own thoughts. She'd returned from Mary's in time to help Jane with supper preparations, and Luke had returned from the creek shortly after.

Pings of silver against china punctuated the silence. Jane tried to eat hurriedly without appearing uncivil. It was a challenge, but the small portions she'd spooned onto her plate expedited the process. She was rising from her chair as Luke was helping himself to seconds.

"Finished already?" The warm smile he offered caused Jane to purse her lips, steeling herself against his charm.

"I'd best get things cleaned up." Jane removed her dinnerware and hurried into the kitchen. A week and five days to go. How was she going to manage?

She pumped water into the basin, using the physical effort as a release for her anxiety. If only she could come down with some minor ailment, then she could return home, and they could find someone to take her place. But such a thing would never happen. She never got sick. Certainly not in the middle of summer. She attacked the dishes with vigor.

Luke appeared suddenly, and she jumped. "Sorry. Apparently, I've startled you again."

Jane noted the contrite look on his face and abruptly turned back to her dishes and clenched her jaw. *I will not let him get to me!*

"I was wondering if you'd like to go for a ride tonight. The sky's clear and it's going to be a beautiful sunset. I think Brownie—"

"Not tonight, Luke."

Jane caught his startled pause and softened her words with an easy excuse. "My back aches from gardening."

Elizabeth clattered a plate down beside the basin and returned to the table with a cloth to wipe it down. Jane snatched the plate, thankful it was the last, and plunked it into the water.

"Why didn't you say so? I have some liniment in the other—"

"I don't need any." Jane hung the wet towel to dry. "I think I'll head on home now."

Elizabeth bade her farewell, but Luke just stood with his hands in his pockets and his brows drawn together in confusion.

છ

Luke just couldn't seem to concentrate tonight. He closed his Bible, leaving it to rest on his lap, and reclined on the upholstered sofa. With his hands behind his head, he drew a deep breath and released it in a puff of frustration.

What was going on with Jane? Sunday morning when

they'd left for church, things had been just fine. She'd laughed with him over breakfast and shared smiles with him on the way to church.

And Saturday night. . . How could he forget Saturday night? He'd almost kissed her, and he was sure—well, almost sure—that Jane would have welcomed it. He'd planned to get to know Jane better; see if their relationship developed into something more.

But something had happened. Ever since she'd come back from her parents' house, she'd been aloof. She acted as though she'd wiped out the past two weeks and reverted to her former behavior. Worse even. She was avoiding him, being snappy with him, and acting as if she didn't care to be near him. And that smarted.

Just when he decided to pursue the relationship, she pulled back and left him fluttering in the wind. *Women!*

Why was she pulling away from him? Perhaps she was worried he still had feelings for Cassy. Maybe she was distancing herself from him to protect herself. He couldn't blame her. Even *he* wasn't sure how he felt about Cassy.

Should he just continue on, hoping she would warm up to him as she did before, or should he ask what was wrong?

I guess you'd better get on your knees, Luke. His lips turned up in a bittersweet smile. His mother's words would live forever in his heart. Clasping the Bible between his hands, Luke eased himself off the couch and obeyed the ageless advice of a wise mother.

twelve

The next week trudged by. On Monday morning, Jane allowed a smile of relief. Only six days to go. Then she could get on with her life.

Her family had proudly shown her through their completed house on Sunday. Even their home in Philadelphia had not been so lovely. The banister was etched with intricate carvings, and the cabinetry was replete with detail. Carpets covered the floors in each room, ready to warm their frigid feet come winter. The fireplace was massive; a grand, stony throne that seemed to encompass the whole parlor. The spacious kitchen, crammed with cubbyholes and drawers for storage, was her mother's pride. Along the outside wall, a big black stove waited quietly to be fired up and used. The house was an impressive structure, and Jane was eager to move in. They'd already moved all their boxes and furniture, and next week she was going to paint the restaurant's name on the big picture window.

A warm bath would be bliss, but there was no time for that this morning. Jane quickly got ready and headed to the Reileys' house. On her way up the porch stairs, she met Elizabeth, who was going to collect the eggs.

"Good morning!" Elizabeth greeted her cheerfully. "Luke's already had breakfast and left, so there's no hurry."

"Why don't we have pancakes, then, since they're your favorite."

119

Elizabeth bounced off to do her chores, and Jane set about making breakfast. By the look of things, she could have had that bath after all.

Luke had missed breakfast several times in the past week, and Jane wondered if his absence had anything to do with her. Probably not. But she felt oddly disappointed each time, when she should've felt relieved.

Suddenly, the truth slammed into her, and the discovery hit her full force. She was in love with him.

Shock turned into anger. Why had she been put in this miserable situation? If she'd never come to stay here, her feelings never would have had a chance to develop. But God had allowed it. He'd put before her something she could never have; dangled it like a bone before a dog. Bad enough that she had to live with herself the way she was, but now she had to suffer unrequited love as well. Did God despise her so much?

Why, God? What did I ever do that was so awful? She slammed a glass down onto the table and cringed at the echo that sounded. *Just six more days,* she told herself, then she could retreat to her parents' house and nurse her broken heart.

੨ð

Monday dragged into Tuesday, which turned out to be another unbearably hot day without so much as a breeze to cool a person's skin. Heavy chores were put off in favor of lighter, outdoor chores. Laundry filled the bill, so Jane and Elizabeth scrubbed and wrung, then hung the clothes to dry on the clothesline, which was as stagnant as a cactus.

Next, Jane and Elizabeth watered the garden. They stirred up dust, which clung to the roofs of their mouths, as they hauled buckets from the pump to the plants. Occasionally, they sprinkled water on each other to fight the heat and provide a little fun. When half of the garden was watered, they sank into the grass under a huge oak and agreed to finish tomorrow.

Supper that night followed the same pattern as the previous week. Jane, feeling Luke's silent perusal, rushed through the meal and cleanup, then retired to the sanctuary of her cottage. After a cool bath in the cabin's tiny kitchen, Jane scooped up her sewing basket and eased herself into the rocker on the porch in hopes of escaping the house's stifling heat.

She was nearly finished with Elizabeth's new dress. Draping the yellow fabric over her shoulder to keep it off the ground, Jane began hemming the gown, leaving a generous three inches for growth.

Tiny, even stitches, the trademark of fine sewing, were produced with little conscious effort. In fact, the tedious work lulled her mind into a dreamlike state.

The slam of a door released her from her stupor, jerking her mind to the present like a fisherman yanking a snared fish. Her eyes followed the sound, and her stomach dropped to her toes when she saw Luke headed her way. She couldn't slink back into the cottage, because he had already spotted her.

Jane continued sewing, determined to pay him as little attention as possible until he took the hint and left her alone.

His feet shuffled to a stop and, when she glanced up, she saw he was lounging casually against the porch rail in front of her, his hands in his pockets.

" 'Evening," he said.

She steeled her heart against his lopsided grin and returned to her task, not even bothering to return his greeting.

"Making yourself a dress?" he asked, irritating her further.

"No. This is for Elizabeth."

"What a shame. That color looks real nice on you."

She heard the smile in his voice and clenched her teeth in frustration. "Is there something you wanted, Luke?"

Luke disregarded her question. "You'd look pretty in a soft color like that. I'm used to seeing you in plain colors."

She stiffened as though he had struck her as the singsong voices from her childhood taunted her, *"Plain Jane. . .plain Jane. . ."* Her mind reeled with images: Bart Matthews slinging mud at her, a group of children snickering as she hurried past, cute little Emily Parker sneering at her.

Jane smothered the images from her mind, but Luke's words chafed at her like a burr against her skin. *Who is he to criticize my clothes? What does he know about fashion, anyway?*

In one motion, Jane scooped up her basket and whirled around to the door. She grasped the handle and gave a yank, but a viselike grip on her arm forestalled her departure. She tried to wrench her arm away, but his hand held firmly, so she let the door swing shut with a bang.

"What? What did I say?" She heard his soft words and felt them, as well, as his breath stirred the wisps of hair near her ear, sending a shiver down her spine.

"Nothing. I–I'm just tired, that's all." She squared her shoulders.

"Something's wrong. What did I say?"

"You didn't say anything," she snapped.

Luke spun her around to face him, and she witnessed his anger for the first time. The planes of his face were hard and forbidding, his eyes alive with emotion. Jane sank back against the door to distance herself from his body, and the knob dug into her spine. The ache in her back matched the one in her arm caused by Luke's grip, and she squirmed. Luke released her abruptly, as if he hadn't realized the strength of his hold.

He exhaled in a puff of frustration. "Then what's wrong, Jane?" he asked between clenched teeth. "You've been avoiding me. Things were fine a week ago, now you can't get far enough away. Did I do something to make you mad?" His eyes searched hers, and Jane dipped her head in guilt.

"No. . .no." She avoided his eyes. "It's not you, it's me. I just want to be left alone."

Silence wove around her, filling up the space between them. Her heart thumped wildly in her chest, betraying her inner turmoil.

"I don't want to leave you alone."

The words, spoken so simply, drew a silent gasp from Jane. Her eyes darted to meet his gaze, and she wanted to melt in the warmth of his eyes. But cold reality stabbed at her, and she hardened herself against his kindness. "I don't need your *pity,* Luke."

He drew back suddenly, as though she'd slapped him. "Pity. . .? I want to spend time with you, get to know you better. I don't pity you." His fingers curved under her trembling chin, and he met her with a direct gaze that went straight to her heart. "I'm beginning to care for you, Jane."

Her eyes glazed over, and she blinked rapidly. What was he saying? Could it be possible that—

"I was planning to tell you after you came back from your parents' house last Sunday, but you were so. . .cold. I don't even know how you feel about this now." Luke dropped his hand. "Am I making a fool of myself?" A red flush climbed up his neck and into his face.

She swallowed, trying to dislodge the hard lump that had formed in her throat. "What about Cassy?" she asked in a monotone voice, afraid to give away her feelings. Afraid she'd somehow misunderstood him.

Luke's face clouded with uneasiness. "I'm going to be honest with you. I'm a little confused about my feelings where she's concerned." He stuffed his hands in his pockets, then met her gaze. "With her being away. . .my feelings for her have. . . I'm not sure how I feel."

Jane felt for him and encouraged him with a slight smile.

After an audible exhale he continued, "The truth is I won't know exactly how I feel about Cassy until she comes back. I don't know why that is. . . . Maybe what I felt for her was shallow." His eyes drilled into hers with passion. "What I do know is, I want to get to know you better, Jane. After you return home, I'd like your permission to call on you."

Jane opened her trembling lips to respond, but closed them again when nothing came out.

"I *have* made a fool of myself, haven't I?" Disappointment lined his face, covered by a shadow of humiliation.

A tight cord knotted inside her stomach, and Jane felt an overwhelming urge to ease his discomfort. "No," she denied emphatically.

Her sudden response drew a startled look from Luke, and her face filled with the white heat of embarrassment. "I mean. . .I would like. . .that is, you may call on me after I return home. If you'd like." Her eyes darted to his in an effort to gauge his response. His eyes were wide in surprise, then they were sparkling and framed by familiar crinkles. His grin widened to a full smile as her words sank in.

"That's great. . .just great," he said with a dazed smile.

Jane removed the dress that was draped across her shoulders and transferred the sewing basket to her other hand. The uncomfortable silence stirred her heart.

"Well. . .here, let me get the door for you." Luke opened the door, and Jane slipped inside, glad to end the awkward moment. "I'll see you in the morning, then," he said.

His intense gaze mesmerized Jane. "All right. Good night." She shut the door, then discreetly watched from the window as he walked away.

Her heart pumped vigorously. *I can hardly believe it,* she thought. *He actually cares for me!* She felt a childish urge to jump up and down, but her mother's persistent training restrained her.

Jane put away her sewing supplies and lit the sitting room lamp. She was in the mood to draw, and she knew just the picture to work on.

છે

The next day dawned bright and warm, the heat of yesterday melting into yet another scorching August day. Clouds lining the horizon hinted at the possibility of rain, and the trees sheltering the two houses whispered secrets to one another as a fine breeze toyed with their branches.

Jane was as nervous as a turkey on Thanksgiving Day as she made her way to the Reiley house. She'd fussed with her appearance, combing her hair into various styles, each more ridiculous than the one before, until finally clasping it back into her usual knot. She was behaving like a silly schoolgirl.

She began her routine in solitude, glad to have the time to collect herself before facing Luke. Elizabeth joined her, and soon breakfast was on the table. Luke slid into his chair, after running late with his morning chores, and offered Jane an intimate smile.

She squirmed in her chair. Luke held out his hands, and Jane and Elizabeth joined theirs to his before he said grace. Jane didn't hear a word. His hand was warm and rough against hers, and for the first time she noticed his hand engulfed hers. Her palms began to sweat, and Jane wished he would hurry.

Just then, she felt his thumb stroke hers with deliberate slowness. Under this gentle assault, her own thumb trembled, tingled with each light touch. His slightest movement sent shivers rippling through the rest of her body until Jane was sure she was going to faint.

With a final squeeze, Luke released her hand, and Jane quickly reclaimed it, while avoiding his eyes. Throughout breakfast, Luke bantered with Elizabeth and attempted to include Jane. Jane tried to act normally but felt as if her laughter was stiff and strained.

How did other women do it? Cassy and Katy made the whole thing seem so effortless. They engaged in clever repartee, lowered their eyelashes at just the right moment, and even blushed at the right time. And they were never tongue-tied. She had observed her sisters with their beaus countless times, and they had never seemed ill at ease—the way she felt now.

Jane struggled through breakfast, ever conscious of Luke's

scrutiny. As much as she wanted to get to know him, she was most eager for his departure so she could relax.

Breakfast finally ended, and Jane heaved a sigh of relief when Luke left. She and Elizabeth began a batch of bread dough. As hot as the day was likely to be, the dough would rise in record time.

Elizabeth had been begging Jane to sketch her, so while the dough rose, Elizabeth found a spot in the shade to pose. She was a perfect model, sitting as still as a sun-bathing turtle. Time passed quickly as the strokes of lead took shape. When she was finished, Elizabeth smiled back from the page, a mischievous tomboy with long braids.

"Oh, I can't wait to show Mary! She'll be so jealous!" Elizabeth said around a giggle.

When they went inside, the bread was ready to be punched down and shaped into loaves. After lunch, Jane showed Elizabeth the dress she had almost completed. With only a little hemming left, Jane turned the task over to Elizabeth to finish, while she scrubbed the floors.

Dinnertime arrived with extraordinary speed, giving Jane no time to fret over seeing Luke. With so little time to prepare the meal, Jane decided on chipped beef, fried potatoes, and slices of fresh bread.

After Luke washed up, they seated themselves at the table and joined hands. Jane held her breath waiting for Luke to repeat this morning's caresses, but her anxiety was for naught.

"Oh, Luke!" Elizabeth said after the prayer. "You should see the picture Jane drew of me today. It looks just like me!"

Jane ducked her head as Luke's gaze skimmed her face. "Well, now, I'd like to have a look at that."

Elizabeth hurriedly swallowed a mouthful of potatoes. "I'll show it to you after supper. Jane is a good drawer." Suddenly her face lit up. "Why don't you draw Luke, too?"

Jane dropped her fork, and it clattered on her plate. "I. . . I don't know, Elizabeth. . ."

"He'd sit real still—wouldn't you, Luke?"

Jane glanced at Luke, and he winked at her, his dimple coming out to play. "I sure would. I'd be the best model you've ever had."

Jane swallowed and sputtered as the food went down the wrong way. She grabbed her glass and gulped down the remainder of her lemonade. When she recovered, she spoke. "I–I don't think—"

Luke's lips twitched. "What? Am I too ugly to draw?"

Elizabeth giggled, and Jane searched for an excuse. Perhaps she could just put it off—indefinitely. "Maybe later I could—"

Elizabeth interrupted. "How 'bout after supper?" She looked from Jane to Luke in expectation.

"Well, I don't know. . . ."

"Sounds great!" they responded simultaneously. Naturally his reply overruled hers.

Luke and Elizabeth resumed eating, and Jane gave a sigh of resignation. How was she going to draw anything with Luke staring at her? She couldn't even carry on an intelligent conversation with him present. If she just admitted she'd already sketched him, she wouldn't have to go through this, but there was no way she was going to admit that! She'd just work quickly.

After supper, Jane's efforts at stalling were made ineffective by Elizabeth's enthusiastic cleaning. All hopes of waiting until the daylight faded were dashed when Elizabeth slapped the wet washcloth over the basin to drain. "Everything's done! I'll go show Luke my picture."

She scurried around the corner, and Jane walked in resignation to the cottage to gather her supplies. Next, she set up two chairs opposite one another on her porch. Thin, wispy clouds covered the low-hanging sun, and she knew from experience this would prevent unnatural shadows from appearing on Luke's face.

She took a seat and perched her drawing pad on her knee. At least Elizabeth would be present for the sitting. Jane wasn't keen on having a spectator while she sketched, but the girl would be a distraction for Luke.

"I'm ready. Where do you want me?"

Jane jumped, and her sketch pad tumbled to the ground. She scrambled to gather the papers, remembering Luke's portrait was among them.

"Didn't mean to startle you." Luke tried to assist Jane, but she was too quick.

"That's okay. Sit over there." She gestured to the Boston rocker, and Luke lowered himself onto the chair and removed his hat. He ran a hand through his wavy brown locks.

"Where's Elizabeth?" Jane balanced her pad on her leg and began a series of strokes that would become the outline of his face.

One side of Luke's mouth tipped up. "I told her it might make you nervous to have her watch. She went to Mary's to play."

Jane's stomach gave a disheartened flop, and her heart rate accelerated. If he only knew—he was the cause of her nervousness. Her hands trembled with each stroke, and she paused a moment, under the guise of studying his face, to collect herself. She drew a deep breath and silently released it.

"What's wrong? Do you want me to sit a different way?"

"What? Oh. No, you're fine."

Luke began a story about one of Caleb's childhood antics. Jane relaxed as he talked, relieved to have the attention diverted from her. She listened to him for a few moments, but then found her attention drawn to Luke's features, his bass voice a pleasant rumble in the background. A stray lock of hair hung rebelliously over his brow and, as she drew it, she found herself longing to brush it away.

Her gaze went continually from Luke, to her paper, then back to Luke again. He tilted his head and smiled in the telling of his story, but Jane knew his features so well that the sketch progressed rapidly. Once the basic outline was in place, Jane spent the majority of the time looking at the sketch: darkening in shadows, giving his hair texture, contouring his cheekbones. She glanced up only periodically to check on lighting details and such. With her index finger, she smudged the lead, blending the shadows to smooth out the lines. Jane looked up at Luke to note the angle of a shadow.

He wasn't there. She gasped when she saw him standing beside her.

Jane clutched the sketch pad to her chest. "I'm not finished yet!"

Luke, his hand on the back of her chair, squatted down until his face was even with hers. His eyes crinkled. "I already saw it. You're quite good, you know." Luke withdrew the pad from her clutches and set it back on her knee.

Jane looked away from Luke, his nearness playing havoc with her senses, and blew gently on the portrait, scattering the particles of dust. She held her breath as Luke quietly studied his picture. What did he think of it? Drawing was such a personal part of her. She wondered if her feelings for him were somehow etched into the lines that depicted his face.

"You flatter me." She heard the smile in his voice and met his warm gaze. "I'm not nearly that handsome."

Jane ducked her head, and heat filled her body, spreading outward toward her limbs.

Luke tilted her chin up with his fingertips. His eyes bore into hers with a strange intensity. "Didn't mean to embarrass you."

Jane, uneasy and apprehensive, tried to turn away, but his fingers did not relinquish their hold. His eyes, burning with fervor, held hers captive. She hardly dared to breathe and, when his gaze dropped to her lips, her breath caught in her throat.

Silence swelled around them, filling every available cranny. Jane was cognizant of only Luke, his beautiful face mere inches from hers. And then the distance dwindled to nothing as his lips met hers. It was a caress, feather-soft and tentative, lasting only a second, but its effect was extensive.

A knot tightened in her stomach as Luke drew away. His eyes, normally alive with laughter, blazed with compelling earnestness. "Maybe I should apologize, but I'm not going to," he said huskily. His lips tilted gently. "You have a smudge right here," he said as he smoothed the blotch away with the pad of his thumb.

Jane turned her head and rubbed at the spot with unsteady hands, unsure of what to say. She could still feel Luke's lips on hers, warm and soft.

"Can I keep the picture?" Luke's voice rumbled in her ear.

"I'm not finished." Jane mechanically went to work on the portrait, glad to give her hands something to do. Her mind was on Luke, still sitting so near, his arm encircling the back of her chair. She made an effort to regulate her shallow breathing.

Luke spoke, his breath tickling her ear. "I guess you could say I have mixed feelings about your going home."

Jane waited for him to finish, but he said nothing, so she spurred him on. "Oh?"

Luke was silent until Jane met his gaze. "I hate that I won't see you every day, but I'm looking forward to courting you."

He was so direct. Jane gulped, then slowly resumed her work, unsure of what to say and unwilling to be so bold as to return the compliment.

"You *are* still going to allow me to call on you?"

Jane gritted her teeth. "Yes." Must she spell it out for him? She'd let him kiss her, for heaven's sake.

She heard a noise and realized Luke was stifling his laughter. "What?" she demanded, pinning him with a glare.

A full-fledged smile appeared, and his twinkling eyes softened. "You know something, Jane? I think I like you."

Jane stiffened her back and tilted her chin, unwilling to soften. "Your picture's finished," she said, extending it in his direction, but keeping her eyes straight ahead.

She felt him kiss her cheek and had to restrain herself from reacting.

"Good night, Jane. See you in the morning."

She heard the smile in his voice, but didn't look his direction until he was walking away. Then she watched him until he disappeared into the house.

❧

That night Jane tossed about on the hard, hay-filled mattress. She was almost used to the uncomfortable bedding by now. No, the mattress wasn't keeping her awake.

Luke was to blame.

She smiled in the private darkness and allowed her mind to review for the umpteenth time the kiss she and Luke had shared. So this was what all the fuss was about! No wonder Cassy had acted so silly over Caleb. She felt like her brain was filled with warm mush, and when Luke was with her, she was never happier. Joy wrapped around her like a warm blanket.

Jane sighed deeply and snuggled into her pillow. Who would have thought anyone would ever care for her? And not just anyone, but Luke. He was so handsome, and so. . . good. Any woman would be lucky to have him, but he cared for *her*. She could hardly fathom it.

And his kiss. Her heart thumped heavily just thinking about it. How could a mere touch elicit such passion? Why, she knew the exchange had hardly lasted a second, yet his kiss had shaken her clear down to her toes. Had he felt that way, too? He'd seemed perfectly calm. *Maybe he regretted it,* she thought for an anxious moment. But, no, he'd said he wasn't sorry. He'd even said he was looking forward to courting her. *Her.* Plain Jane Cooper.

thirteen

The next day, they fixed and served breakfast in typical fashion, then Luke left with his rifle and a promise to bring home some game. That morning Jane had felt like a housewife for the first time, fixing breakfast for Luke and Elizabeth. She'd been doing it nearly four weeks now, but with Luke gazing at her from across the table, it was easy to pretend he was her husband and Elizabeth her daughter.

She mentally scolded herself as she hung the wet laundry. He had barely even begun to show an interest in her, and she was dreaming of being his wife. Yet, here she stood performing the intimate task of washing and hanging his undershorts. It was an odd situation, to be sure. At least when she returned home, they could begin courting like a normal couple, and they would have the advantage of already knowing one another quite well.

"Can we go riding after lunch, Jane?" Elizabeth asked.

"I guess we may as well. The laundry won't be dry for a while, even with the wind." Jane was glad to feel competent enough to ride a horse. She was no equestrian, that was for certain, but it felt good to have conquered one of her biggest fears.

After lunch, Elizabeth helped Jane saddle their horses, and then they started off, following the western border of the property. As they rode, Elizabeth told Jane about the dolls she and Mary were making. Twin dolls, with matching pinafores and golden yarn for hair. Jane smiled at Elizabeth's enthusiasm.

Jane's back was beginning to ache by the time they'd crossed the vast prairie and entered the heavily wooded grove. She was about to suggest they turn back when Elizabeth pointed through the thick copse of trees.

"Look, there's Luke."

Sure enough, through the thick foliage, relaxing with his back against the base of a tree about fifty yards away was Luke. His horse was tied to a nearby tree. Jane and Elizabeth turned their horses toward him.

Elizabeth giggled. "So this is what he does all day. Let's sneak up on him!"

Jane met Elizabeth's gaze and smiled at her in conspiracy. There was only the rustle of the wind through the trees to disguise their approach, so they agreed to dismount and approach on foot.

Elizabeth dismounted her horse, watching Luke with an impish gleam in her eye. Jane had just started to swing her leg around, when she saw Elizabeth's expression change, her mouth dropping in horror. Her eyes widening in terror. Jane glanced toward Luke, but the heavily wooded area shielded him from her view.

It all happened at once. A scream. A fierce cracking sound.

Then all she knew was panic when Brownie bolted with lightning speed through the woods. Balanced with one foot on the stirrup, Jane instinctively clung to the horse. Her right foot searched for the elusive stirrup.

Branches clawed at her face and body, threatening to rip her from the saddle. Her foot gave up its futile search and instead hugged the massive body that seemed intent on unseating her. Jane hunched down low, clutching a handful of mane in one hand and the saddle horn in the other.

God, help me! The words exploded in her mind repeatedly as she struggled with all her strength to maintain her precarious balance. Jolts assaulted her body. She grunted as the wind was knocked from her stomach. Brownie dodged left and right, narrowly missing overhanging branches.

Screams pierced the wooded sanctuary, echoing eerily off the trees. Suddenly the light blinded her as Brownie darted from the darkness of the forest to the flat plain of the prairie. She felt her body shift to the right as the crazed horse launched to the left. She was going to fall. . . . She couldn't hang on much longer!

The strides lengthened with speed, but her balance was gone. *Oh, God, help me!* There was one last jolt as Brownie cleared a ditch. She went flying through the air. In a flash she saw a fence and the ground racing toward her. She flung out her hands in desperation. Then, mercifully, oblivion claimed her.

❧

Luke sank down against the huge oak and rested his rifle across his lap. Moments ago he'd sighted the buck he'd been trailing for the last thirty minutes, but before he could get the gun to his shoulder it had disappeared through the foliage. He was sure it had gone this way, and he was willing to wait as long as it took.

His ears pricked when he heard leaves crunching. He turned his head sideways, listening intently for the rustling. There it was again. Off to his right. He quietly raised the rifle to his shoulder and aimed it in the direction of the noise. Within seconds he saw the telltale brown hide. With expertise, he sighted the beast down the barrel of his gun and squeezed the trigger.

A scream pierced the woods. Panic ripped through him. Chills shot down his spine. "Dear God!" Luke leaped to his feet and scrambled in the direction of his shot. Before he'd covered a few feet, he spotted them. Brownie plunged through the woods, and Jane was hanging on frantically. *Oh, dear God! Did I shoot her?*

Elizabeth stood beside her horse, her hands covering her mouth.

Luke scrambled to untie Maizy, then vaulted on. He snapped her into a gallop, dodging limbs as he went, wishing frantically he'd chosen a faster mount that morning. As soon as he cleared the woods, he saw Brownie's dashing figure and nudged his horse into a full run.

Jane's frantic screams were carried to him by the wind. "Come on, girl, go!" he urged. His eyes pinned on Jane, the distance slowly dwindled. But to his horror, he saw her slipping sideways in the saddle. "Hang on, Jane!" *Please, God, keep her safe!*

When he saw Brownie shoot over the gully, he knew. The scene played out cruelly in slow motion as the jolt hurled Jane through the air. Her body flew like a rag doll, her limbs outstretched. Luke watched helplessly as she tangled with the fence before finally hitting the ground with a thud.

"JANE!" The words tore from his mouth in desperation. "Oh, God, please let her be all right!"

He leaped to the ground before his horse reached a full stop. Barbed wire clawed at his skin as he scrambled over the fence. But he felt no pain.

Jane lay in a heap facedown, her body as lifeless as a sack of grain. When he reached her, he gently rolled her over.

The bodice of her dress was ripped. Blood trickled down her face from a gash that ran from her cheek to her shoulder. Her brown dress was stained red. *Oh, God, tell me I didn't shoot her!* He didn't see any bullet holes, but couldn't take the time to examine her thoroughly. His pulse thudded in his ears, deafening him to the world.

He scooped her up in his arms and somehow got across the fence. Elizabeth rode up as he was setting Jane atop his horse.

"Is she okay?" she screamed, her eyes wild with fear.

"I don't know! She's bleeding! I'm taking her to Doc Hathaway's!"

"I'm coming, too!"

"No! Find Brownie and take her back to the stable!"

There was no time for more words. Luke mounted behind Jane's limp body and nudged Maizy into a full run. He cradled her to his chest with one arm, his hand resting on the damp bodice of her dress.

The ride was interminable. He prayed aloud in fragmented sentences. Not once did Jane stir. An ugly knot had formed on her forehead, as had bruises of every shape and color. The gash across her face continued to seep blood.

Luke snapped the reins hard. "Yah! Yah!" he encouraged the winded horse.

At last, he reached town and spurred his mount down the dusty road. *Be there, Doc!* he pleaded.

He reined in when he reached the building that housed

the doctor's office. "Doc!" he called, sliding off the horse and easing Jane into his arms.

Doc Hathaway appeared at the door. "What happened?" he asked as he held the door open for Luke.

"I fired my rifle. . . . I don't know if I shot her. . . . It spooked her horse. . . ."

"Lay her on the table in there!" He gestured to the small room separated from the office by a gray curtain, then scurried to the basin and washed his hands.

Luke laid his precious load on the table. She moaned and turned her head, but her eyes remained closed. "It's all right, Jane," he whispered. "You're going to be fine."

The doctor rushed into the room. "Wait out there, Luke," he said as he placed a stethoscope on her chest.

Everything in him told him to stay, but he backed away from the table and slipped behind the curtain. He paced the tiny office, his long stride making short work of the space. His breath poured out of his lungs, and he fought the tears that welled up in his eyes. *If I shot her, I'll never forgive myself! How could I have been so stupid? Even a tenderfoot knows the difference between a deer and a horse!*

Luke stopped short in the edge of the worn, oval carpet. *What am I doing?*

Immediately, he dropped to his knees, assuming the position that always humbled him before the Lord. With his face buried in his hands, he took a moment to collect his thoughts and still the wild thumping in his chest. Then he began to pray.

Oh, Father in heaven, please help Jane to be all right! Don't let her suffer for my mistake! I know You care about her even more than I do, and You must know what a special lady she is. Please touch her body with Your healing hands.

Luke continued to share his heart with God. He didn't know how long he'd been on his knees when he heard the whisper of the curtain opening.

He shot to his feet. "Is she going to be all right?"

Doc Hathaway drew the curtain closed and came to stand next to Luke. "Well, she didn't take a gunshot wound, so that much is good news."

Luke exhaled a breath he didn't know he'd been holding.

"However," the doctor continued, "she has sustained two injuries that have me concerned. There's a nasty bump on her head, from a fall off the horse, I'm assuming?"

Luke nodded his head, and the doctor continued. "It's hard to say how serious that injury is. She does have a concussion, but we won't know the extent of the damage, if any, until she comes around. Did she regain consciousness at all on your way here?"

"No, no, I don't think so. What about the other injury?" Luke's head throbbed at his temples, and he blinked to force himself to concentrate.

"There's a cut that runs from the side of her face down to her shoulder. It was fairly deep, and she's lost a lot of blood. I sutured it, but the loss of blood concerns me."

Luke drew a shaky breath and forced the words. "She'll make it, won't she?"

The doctor drew in a deep breath, puffing his chest out, then squinted his bespectacled eyes. "I think she will, though, as I said, we'll have a better idea of how she is after she regains consciousness."

"Her family. I need to let them know. . . ."

ॐ

Jane felt the pain before she even opened her eyes. Her head throbbed as it never had before, and there was a deep ache in her face and shoulder. *What is wrong with me?* She lifted her trembling hand to touch the source, but it fell heavily on the bed before reaching its destination.

ॐ

She opened her eyelids, but the darkness didn't retreat. She turned her head slowly on the pillow and was rewarded with a stab of pain. She groaned. Slowly the room came into focus, and she saw it was nighttime beyond the little window to her right. Indistinct shapes of furniture lined the walls of the unfamiliar room. *Where am I?* She closed her eyes against the savage pain in her head. Suddenly, her whereabouts didn't matter.

ॐ

Voices. *A woman's,* she thought. She struggled through the hazy fog that enveloped her, but couldn't seem to find her way out. . . .

"Jane? Jane, wake up!"

She tried to open her eyes, but they were too heavy.

"That's it, darling, open your eyes. You can do it!"

The light bombarded her eyes, and she quickly shut them again. She moaned in response to the drums beating in her head.

"Jane, you must open your eyes! Katy, go fetch the doctor!"

Mama. Jane made another effort, lifting a hand to shield her eyes from the overwhelming sunlight. Her mother's face swam before her eyes. "Mama. . ."

"Yes, darling, you're going to be all right."

"My head."

"You have a concussion, but the doctor said you'd be fine. We've been so worried!"

"What day is this?"

"Thursday. The accident was yesterday. Do you remember what happened?"

Jane drew her hand away from her face, trying to become accustomed to the light. "The horse bolted. . . . I couldn't hold on."

"Yes, Luke told us all about it. He feels perfectly awful. Thinks it's all his fault."

Jane wanted to object, but her strength was rapidly draining. She heard a door slam, then Dr. Hathaway bustled through a curtain hanging just beyond her mother.

"Well, now, my patient awakens! Let's see how we're doing today. . . ."

After asking her some questions and examining her eyes and head, the doctor smiled down at her. "I think you're going to be just fine. You'll have to rest and take your time in recovering and, of course, I'll need to remove the sutures later.

What sutures? Jane wondered. The doctor addressed her mother.

"There's no reason why you can't take her home, Mrs. Cooper. She'll be more comfortable there, and you'll be able to. . ."

Jane tried to cling to the voice, but the dark fog dragged her under once again.

fourteen

The next time Jane awoke, she felt like a bear coming out of hibernation: still groggy, but ready to join the world. She glanced around the room until her gaze settled on someone knitting in the rocker across the room. *Katy.* Her sister rushed to her side. Had she spoken the name aloud?

Katy's soft hand grasped her own. "Jane, how do you feel? Oh, how silly of me! You feel wretched, of course. Can I get you anything? A drink? Are you hungry?"

Under other circumstances, Jane would have smiled at her sister's typical babbling, however, her physical pain dulled her sense of humor. "Where's Mama?"

Katy tucked a blond curl behind her ear. "She's downstairs in the restaurant, but she wanted me to come fetch her when you awoke. Will you be all right for a minute? Let me get you some water first." She filled a glass with water from the porcelain pitcher, then helped Jane sit up to take a sip.

Pain exploded in Jane's head at the movement, but a powerful thirst gave her the determination to finish the glass.

"I'll be right back." The door whooshed shut.

Jane put a hand to the front of her head where it throbbed. A bandage covered the area, but she felt a large swollen lump just under its surface. Next, she glanced down to her left shoulder to explore the tightening pain coming from that area. Sutures. A jagged line of tiny stitches ran up her shoulder and disappeared from her line of vision.

She raised her hand to her face again, this time to probe the discomfort along the side of her face. Her fingers found the bumpy, raised ridge that started at the hollow of her cheek. She followed the line down her jaw, where it broke for an inch or so, then continued along her neck to the sutures she'd found on her shoulder.

Not my face, too! Tears of frustration welled up in her eyes. She would be scarred! She remembered the scar David had on his arm from a childhood mishap with a saw blade. Its stark whiteness still stood out in contrast against his dark skin. *Aren't I homely enough already, God? Now, I'll look like a freak!*

Anna Cooper slipped into the room, carefully balancing a wooden tray in her nimble hands. Her gaze slid perceptively over Jane's face as she set her burden down on the bedside table. Jane watched the broth slosh over the edge of the soup bowl and pool next to the spoon.

"Katy said you seemed more alert this time. She was right. You look like you might be ready for some food, hmm?" The bed sank a bit as Anna gently settled on the edge. "You gave us quite a scare, young lady."

Jane scanned her mother's face for a clue to her appearance, but received no useful information. "Mama, bring me a mirror."

As if she hadn't heard, Anna lifted the corner of Jane's bandage. "Swelling's gone down. It looks much better." She shared a brief smile as she replaced the white gauze. "Let me feed you some soup. It's best if you start with something light. It's been almost two days since you've had anything, you know. You must be starving. Does your head hurt terribly? The doctor gave us some powders to—"

"Mama, get me a mirror."

Her mother's hand stopped in its path, the spoonful of broth quivering in its pocket. "I will, Jane, but first you're going to finish this soup. Your body needs nourishment to recover."

Her mother's expression and emphatic tone brooked no room for debate, so Jane complied. The broth was hot and tasty, and her taste buds awakened to the flavor. When she was finished, her stomach cried out for more, but Jane ignored it. Her mother held a glass of lemonade to her mouth, and Jane sipped from it. Once the empty dishes were placed on the tray, Jane attempted to prop herself up. Her mother quickly fluffed up the pillows behind her.

"How bad is it?" Jane asked.

"You're going to be just fine." Her mother patted her hand and smiled. "You do have a concussion and a nasty lump on your head, but the doctor says you'll be just—"

"That's not what I mean. How bad does it look?"

Her mother looked momentarily confused. "Why, you're bruised of course. You took a nasty fall. Luke said you tangled with some barbed wire and—"

"I'd like that mirror now." Jane averted her eyes.

"Of course."

Footsteps tapped across the newly polished wood floor, then the drawer of the bureau slid out with a familiar squeak. Jane drew in a shaky breath and let it out with a quiet huff. Shortly, her mother returned. Jane accepted the mirror with a trembling hand and held it up. Her eyes met those in the glass.

Her face was a horrible palette of color. Yellow, blue,

red. The white bandage streaked across her head like a crooked hat, hiding who knows what beneath it. She turned her face to the side. The ugly jagged line slashed down her face and onto her shoulder. She sucked in a breath. The tiny stitches looked unnatural on the skin. Like a delicate satin dress sewn with twine. Her eyes filled with tears, and the hand holding the mirror dropped lifelessly to her lap.

"I'm a freak."

"Jane!" She heard her mother's shock but did not care. "Of course you're not! You're just bruised, that's all. Why, in a week or two you'll be back to normal."

Normal! A strangled laugh escaped her cracked lips. As if that was something wonderful! She met her mother's eyes. The woman looked at Jane as if questioning her sanity.

"I won't look normal, Mama. I'll have a ghastly scar running down my face for everyone to gawk at! You know I will! As if I weren't already—" Jane clamped her mouth shut. Somewhere outside a saw roared to life. Noises from the restaurant filtered through the walls, filling the silence.

"As if you weren't already what?"

Jane struggled to control her rapid breathing. Her head was throbbing again, and she squeezed her eyes shut. Suddenly, she was so tired. . . .

The door clicked open, and Katy stuck her head inside. "Luke's downstairs, Jane. I told him you were awake, and he'd like to see you."

"No!" The word shot out with more vehemence than she'd intended. She couldn't let Luke see her this way. How he'd pity her! "I'm tired, Katy. . . ."

Mama squeezed her hand but addressed her sister. "Katy,

please tell Luke that Jane is doing much better, but has tired out and isn't up for company just yet."

After Katy left, Mama smiled gently at Jane. "He's been hovering around every spare minute. First at the doctor's office, then here." Her mother pulled up the covers and tucked them carefully around Jane. "I get the feeling he cares a great deal for you."

Jane cringed inwardly. "Please Mama, I'm too tired to—"

"I'm sorry, sweetie. I'll send Katy up to sit with you. Is there anything I can get?"

Jane shook her head slowly, too sleepy to answer. She heard the door snap shut, then sank into a dreamless sleep.

&

With the next day came an improvement in her physical condition. Dr. Hathaway came by and pronounced her well enough to sit up and move about a bit. Jane's days were still confused, but her mother told her the accident had been on Wednesday and today was Friday. Cassy and Caleb would be coming home tomorrow. She wondered how Elizabeth and Luke were faring.

Despite being declared fit, Jane's mood was as gray and stormy as the weather. She had never had anything to be vain about, but the thought of her current appearance frightened her more than she was willing to admit.

At the very core of her fear, she realized, were her feelings for Luke. Knots tightened in her stomach every time she imagined Luke seeing her this way. Things had been going so well—better than she had ever dreamed.

And now, *this*. She raised a hand to her face and ran her fingers along the now-familiar ridge. Luke would probably act as if nothing were different. He would avoid looking at it, look into her eyes, and pretend the grotesque deformity wasn't there. He would call on her just as he'd promised. Court her.

Pity her.

How she hated that word! She would rather be laughed at and ridiculed than pitied. But Luke was too nice for that.

He had come by again this afternoon, bringing Elizabeth with him. When she'd made her excuses to her mother again, her mother had searched her face until Jane had averted her eyes. Jane had held her breath, afraid her mother would insist on a brief visit, but finally her mother had sighed and left the room. What would she say the next time?

❧

Jane could no longer deny she was feeling much better. Her headache was now only a dull throb and, though she hadn't dared to look in a glass again, she could tell the swelling was down on her face and head. She wondered if the bruising had faded to a yellow-green yet.

Lying about in bed was becoming a bore. The rocker provided a change of position, but her mind was growing stagnant with nothing to do. Her mother and Katy brought everything she needed, and visits from her father and David provided a change of pace. She desperately wanted out of this room.

But that would be even worse. Well-wishers would gawk at her. And worse, she would have to face Luke. Perhaps since Cassy and Caleb were returning home today, he would be too preoccupied to make the trip to town. He hadn't missed a day yet.

The doctor had come again and said she was healing

quite nicely and should feel like getting up and around soon. The sutures, he'd said, would come out next week. She could hardly wait.

Jane padded back to the bed and sank into its comforting softness. She'd just pulled up the light quilt to her waist and fluffed up the pillows behind her when she heard a tapping on the door. She smiled, recognizing the firm raps of her father's hand.

"Come in, Papa," she called. "It's about time you—"

She froze in horror as Luke's frame filled the doorway.

fifteen

Jane snapped her head toward the window, hiding her face from him. "Go away, Luke!"

The silence lengthened between them, enveloping the room. *What will I do if he comes near?*

"Jane, I just wanted to see for myself—"

"Well, now you've seen. I don't want company." Tension stretched between them like an invisible cord.

His feet shuffled near.

"Jane, what's—"

"Just go! Go, Luke!" Her heart hammered in the taut moments of silence, sending darts of pain through her head. Her words had been harsh, rude even, but at least he'd stopped his approach. She closed her eyes. *Go away! Please, just go away!* her heart pleaded.

The moment suspended in the weighted air. Jane's heart thumped in panic, in tempo with clattering dishes from the kitchen below.

"All right, Jane. Have it your way." His soft voice was like a caress to her ears.

Jane heard his retreating steps, heard the click of the door as it closed, and sank into the bedding. Moments later, through the gauzy curtain, Jane watched Luke mount his horse and ride away.

≈

Luke settled into the worn saddle and nudged his sorrel into motion. His mind had turned numb, so he let his mount carry him home without benefit of guidance.

She blamed him. Her message couldn't have been clearer.

And of course, she was right. Who could dispute the fact that his negligence had spooked her horse? Shooting at a horse. Land's sake, what kind of idiot was he? He'd known to take better care with his target since he'd been knee-high. Who knew what price Jane would pay for his stupidity? How could he deny he was to blame?

He'd seen the sutures on her face in that brief moment before she'd turned away. The wound had been impossible to miss. It would fade in time, maybe disappear completely. Even if it didn't, she would always be beautiful in his eyes. He'd just been relieved she was going to be all right. So relieved, he'd never considered she would blame him as much as he blamed himself. No wonder she had refused to see him. She hadn't been overtired at all. Her mother and sister were just too polite to tell him the truth.

Luke heaved a sigh and pulled down the brim of his felt hat, shielding his eyes from the sun. At least Cassy and Caleb were returning today. The distraction was just what he needed. And maybe Cassy could help Jane forgive him. The Lord knew he would never have intentionally hurt her. Surely Jane knew that.

❧

"Jane?" Mrs. Cooper peeked through the door, then opened it wider and entered the room.

"What is it, Mama?"

The older woman settled on the edge of the mattress and smoothed Jane's hair back from her face. "I saw Luke leave. He seemed upset. I thought perhaps you and he might visit a while. He's been so concerned about you, and I know he was eager to see you."

Jane turned away. "I'm really tired just now, Mama. . . ."

Mrs. Cooper stood abruptly. "I'm dreadfully weary of hearing that."

Jane started to speak, but her mother cut her off. "I know you've been through an ordeal the last few days, but you never seem tired unless the subject of Luke comes up."

"Mama. . . ."

"No, Jane. Your sister and I have been making excuses to Luke for days now. I thought perhaps if I just sent him up, you'd get over whatever's eating at you, but apparently I was wrong."

Jane bowed her head. She had been using her mother and sister as a buffer between herself and Luke, and that wasn't fair. "I'm sorry. I didn't mean to put you and Katy in the middle. I just don't want to see him, that's all."

Her mother's voice softened. "I don't want to pry, but Luke looked so sad as he left, I got the feeling you've broken his heart." Jane felt her mother's fingers gently lifting her chin until their eyes met. "Is that it, darling? You don't return his feelings, and being around him has become awkward?"

Jane shrunk away from her mother in surprise. "No, Mama, that's not it at all."

"Then it's a lovers' quarrel. . . ?"

"No."

Mrs. Cooper let out a puff of breath. "Well, for goodness' sake, Jane, what in the world is it?"

Jane snapped her head toward the window and clamped her jaw tight. Her mother would never understand. She'd been born beautiful. Jane's father had told them many times the story of when they'd met at a cotillion. All the young men had been vying for her mother's attention. "You wouldn't understand."

"Try me."

Jane's gaze snapped back to her mother's as a swift shadow of anger swept through her. "Look at me, Mama! I'm scarred for life. Heaven knows I was never anything to look at, but look at me now! Why did God make me like this? How could He let this happen? No one will ever want me for their wife, much less Luke." Jane twisted the coverlet with strong fingers, barely registering her mother's shock. "Maybe Luke was interested in me before, but there's no way he could ever be now! He'll only pity me, and I'd rather have nothing than have that." Jane saw tears trembling on her mother's lashes and felt a moment of regret. "I want to be alone, Mama. Please."

The bedside window drew Jane's gaze but, as she waited for her mother to leave, she saw nothing beyond the clear glass. The dark cloud that had weighed on her cleared, leaving Jane sorry she'd spoken so harshly. Finally, she heard her mother's soft footsteps and the click of the door as it closed behind her.

She angrily brushed away the moisture on her face, feeling the rough line of sutures. *Why, God? Why did this have to happen? Just as I was beginning to accept myself. Just as I had fallen in love with a man who accepted me for who I am.*

What was she to do with her life now? She could never be content as an old maid now that she'd experienced the joy of love. And yet, no one would want her now. Not even Luke. She threw the covers away from her body, suddenly feeling very hot.

Heavy footsteps sounded along the corridor outside her room, then the door flew open, and her mother stood rigidly in the doorway. Her expression was as stern as Jane had ever seen it, the laugh lines around her face gone smooth and her mouth a tight line of anger.

Jane straightened against the headboard and pulled the cover back up, feeling much like a child about to be reprimanded.

"I have a few things to say to you, Daughter, and I want you to listen closely." She stepped into the room and closed the door behind her. Jane eyed her warily. "I can honestly say I've never been as disappointed in any of my children as I am right now. Do you know how fortunate you are, Jane Cooper?"

Her voice grew louder, and Jane stared in shock as her gentle mother unleashed her anger. "You could have died a few days ago! Your father and I were scared half to death and pleaded for God's mercy on your behalf. You should be thanking God, as we are, that you're alive at all!"

A wave of shame washed over her. She pulled up the quilt and clutched it with a tight fist.

"You're worried about Luke pitying you, but you have pitied yourself enough for everybody!" Her mother stepped closer and crossed her arms. "You have so much to be thankful for, Jane. You're alive, you're healthy, you have a family who loves you, a young man who, by all appearances, cares very much for you, and yet you pity yourself for a disfigurement that may disappear in weeks!"

Jane's gaze fell to her lap, unable to meet her mother's eyes any longer.

"I can think of dozens of people who are worse off than

you. Remember Miss Wharton, back in Philadelphia? Born with a crippling disease and never able to walk even a single step! And that Earnheart boy who fell to his death from his horse? And Mr. Tackett, having that terrible mishap in the mill and losing his hand!"

A fog smothered Jane, seeping into the corners of her heart, filling her with shame. A moment's silence ensued until Jane thought she'd burst from the tension. She didn't dare meet her mother's eyes, having not had such a setdown in all her life.

Her mother exhaled on a sigh, and her voice gentled. "God made you so special, Jane. With amazing talent and formidable strength and, yes, beauty."

Jane's gaze shot to her mother's as denial lumped in her throat.

Her mother held up a hand to ward off her daughter's words. "I know you don't believe it, but you *are* beautiful. I've never seen anyone try so hard to hide their God-given attributes as you do. I've sensed you drifting from God for years now, and I don't know what caused it, but I do know God wants you back. He wants a close relationship with you. And maybe when you draw closer to Him, you'll see yourself through His eyes and see how truly lovely you are."

A shiver danced up her spine as the words penetrated her stubborn heart. When Jane remained silent, her mother walked to the door, then turned on the threshold. "God doesn't look on our outward appearances. He looks on our hearts." With those words, she slipped quietly out the door.

Jane released the blanket, her knuckles aching from the clenching hold, and turned to stare out the window. There had been a time when she'd been close to God, but it was so long ago. How had she come this far away from His presence? Her drifting had happened so slowly, she hadn't even been aware it was happening.

I do want to be close again, Lord. Words jammed in her mind. It had been so long since she'd prayed. *I don't like who I've become. Help me to see myself through Your eyes, beyond the flaws.* With sudden clarity, Jane realized she'd been angry. Not just at her circumstances, but with God Himself. *I'm sorry for blaming You and for my ungrateful spirit.*

Her gaze darted across the room to where Katy's Bible rested on the bureau. How much time had passed since she'd opened the Word outside of church? How silly she'd been. What relationship could survive without communication?

She eased her legs over the side of the bed and retrieved the Bible. Seating herself in the desk chair, she opened the Book to the first chapter of Matthew and began reading. She'd never read Matthew straight through and, as she saw Jesus go from a babe in swaddling clothes to a grown man, her heart identified with Him. His own people rejected Him. Spat upon, cursed, and crucified. The rejections she'd faced paled in comparison.

And He endured it all for her. Tears welled in her eyes as she realized anew God's incredible sacrifice. He'd died for her, and that alone made her worth something. Worth the cost of God's own Son.

She didn't know how long she'd sat there reading and praying, but when she stood again, her childhood commitment had been renewed.

She wanted to do something. She was tired of laying in bed, feeling sorry for herself. With newfound energy, she approached the armoire and selected a gray gown. She'd just finished dressing when a light tap sounded at the door. Wanting to surprise her visitor, she strode to the door and swung it open. "Cassy!"

The sisters embraced, and then Cassy followed Jane into the room and shut the door.

"I was so worried when Luke told us what happened. Don't you know you could've been killed? And what were you doing on that horse anyway? Luke feels just awful, and Mama told me you weren't coping well, but I get here, and you have a big grin on your face."

Jane chuckled at her sister's babbling. Some things never changed. "So much has happened, Cassy. Come sit down, and I'll tell you all about it."

After Jane had summarized the last four weeks, including her feelings about Luke, and her own self-doubt, she relived the accident, telling Cassy all she remembered. Sympathy lined Cassy's face when Jane told how she'd struggled with the disfigurement and how she'd turned Luke away.

"He thinks you blame him, you know," Cassy said.

"What?" Hot prickles of shock coursed through her.

"He told Caleb and me what happened, but he blames himself for the accident. And after you turned him away, he thought you blamed him, too."

"But I don't!" Jane felt an overwhelming need to release him from guilt. "I just felt so ugly, even before the scar, but after. . .I didn't think he could possibly come to love me. And I didn't want him to court me out of pity."

Cassy put her hand along Jane's jaw. "Oh, Jane, you were *never* ugly! You have so much potential, but it's as if you're trying to hide it with that ghastly tight bun and those tiresome clothes. Why, if you made just a little effort, you'd see how pretty you are."

The disbelief that seized her must have shown on her face.

"Let me help you, please, Jane? I can show you how to fix your hair, and we'll make you some colorful dresses. . . ."

Jane smiled at her sister's enthusiasm as she rambled on, planning two new frocks, from the ribbons right down to the thread color.

"Just wait until Luke sees you!" Cassy paused a moment, a secret smile playing on her lips. "I think he loves you."

Jane's breath caught. She'd hoped his courting would bring about strong feelings for her, but love? Could Luke possibly love the woman she'd been?

Suddenly, weariness overcame her, and she noticed her fingers trembling from exhaustion. "I'm so tired all of a sudden. And I haven't even asked you about your honeymoon."

Cassy smiled contentedly. "I'll tell you all about our adventures tomorrow. Mother invited Caleb and me over for dinner after church, as well as Luke and Elizabeth. How about if I come up afterward and fix you up?"

"All right. No, wait! I want to go to church."

"Are you sure you're up to it?"

"Positive."

"Then I'll come over early, and we'll fix you up! Won't Luke be surprised when he sees you at church? You'd better get some rest now."

Cassy placed a kiss on her sister's cheek, and within moments she saw herself out as Jane sank into a pleasant, dream-filled state.

sixteen

The next morning Cassy arrived before daylight, but before she'd been there two minutes, she disappeared from the room. Minutes later she returned with shears in one hand and a gown in the other.

Jane's eyes widened, and she clutched her hair protectively. "You're going to cut my hair?"

Cassy set down the gown and settled her fists on her hips. "Have some faith, Jane. I've never ruined my hair or Katy's."

Jane silently acquiesced. She was right. Besides, what did she have to lose? Her hair couldn't look much worse than it did now. She peered into the mirror, taking one last look at herself before sitting on the chair that Cassy had set across the room. She draped a cloth around her shoulders and began snipping.

Lengths of brown hair floated to the floor as Cassy worked on the sides. "After I'm finished cutting, I'll curl these pieces around your face. How much do you want me to take off the back?"

"Do you have to shorten it?" Something about seeing a part of her falling to the floor made her apprehensive.

"You always wear your hair up anyway, so what difference will it make? Anyway, the shorter length will be easier to manage, and you won't believe how much weight it'll take off your head!"

"All right, but no shorter than midback. And that gown you brought will never work. I'm a good four inches taller than you; it won't even cover my ankles."

"That's not my gown, it's yours."

"I've never owned a periwinkle gown."

Cassy moved to her back. "I made the dress for you. I started weeks ago but put the project on hold while we were planning the wedding. Last night, I took it home and finished the hemming."

Her sister's thoughtfulness warmed her. She turned her head and met her gaze. "I really appreciate this, Cassy."

She was rewarded with a teeth-baring smile. "I'm having as much fun as you are, Jane." Cassy leveled a mock glare. "Now turn around and sit still so I can do my job."

When her hair was cut, Cassy had her slip into the gown, but refused to allow Jane to look in the mirror. "Not yet. I want you to get the full effect."

Next, she put curls around her face, then pulled her hair up loosely. At first, Jane balked at the ribbon that Cassy started to tie in place. She didn't want to overdo it. But, she finally relented at her sister's argument. "Every young woman I know wears ribbons in her hair, why should you be any different?"

The sun was well over the horizon by the time her hair was finished. When Jane tried to rise from the chair and go to the mirror, Cassy stopped her with a hand on her shoulder. "Just a minute."

Jane sighed impatiently. "What now, for goodness' sake?"

Cassy pinched her cheeks.

"Ow! What was that for?"

Her sister giggled and continued to pinch, being careful

to avoid the sutures. "Oh, the price of beauty. Just putting the blush in your cheeks. Now bite your lips."

Jane barely suppressed the urge to roll her eyes, but did as directed. Next, Cassy applied powder to conceal the yellowish bruises.

"That's it—perfect." She rearranged a few curly strands, then straightened the ruffles around the collar. "All right. Go look."

Jane walked on shaky legs to the bureau mirror. This was the moment of truth. Would she look better than she had yesterday, or would she only be disappointed when she saw her reflection? Her stomach clenched in nervous anticipation.

She reached the bureau and lifted her lashes to examine her image. Jane drew in a quick gasp. The difference was . . .indescribable. Her face was mostly the same; her sister hadn't done much there. But somehow the wisps of hair now framing her face brought out her almond-shaped eyes. Her new bangs showed off the arch of her brows and hid the raised bump on her forehead.

And her skin exuded a pinkish glow. Not just where Cassy had pinched, but all over.

"Doesn't that color bring out your lovely skin tone?"

"I can hardly believe my eyes." Jane turned sideways, keeping her gaze on the mirror, studying her hair. The ringlets atop her head made her look feminine and softer.

The dress was a perfect fit. She twirled and watched the skirts float around her.

Cassy giggled. "I used one of your dresses for the measurements. Not bad, I must say."

"It's perfect. And the bodice. . .makes me look more. . ."

"Shapely? With a few tucks and lace, a woman can do remarkable things to fool the eye." She put an arm around Jane and smiled at her in the mirror. "See, Jane. You *are* pretty; you just didn't know it."

"Girls!" Mrs. Cooper called from downstairs. "Time for breakfast, get a move on."

Jane gave her sister one last squeeze, then the two went to join their family. She could hardly wait to see their reactions, but more than anything, she hoped Luke would like her new look.

ૐ

Luke settled against the wagon seat, allowing the two bays to lead the way to church. By now the horses needed little direction, as the only place they ever went was into town. Beside him, Elizabeth was uncharacteristically quiet, an incident he didn't welcome since it gave him too much time to dwell on unpleasant matters.

Jane.

His heart ached with defeat. That and something even worse. Guilt. How could he ask Jane to forgive him when he couldn't forgive himself? If the scars never faded, they would be a constant reminder of his carelessness. One she'd see every time she looked in a mirror. Surely she could never bring herself to forgive him.

He'd struggled over the Coopers' invitation to dinner this afternoon. He couldn't bear to face Jane again. But since she hadn't stepped out of her room since she'd been brought there, he figured there was no sense in turning the offer down. He could avoid her today, but he couldn't avoid her forever. They'd see each other at church and around town. And now they were practically related. He'd see her every time the families got together. See her and long for her, all the while feeling responsible for his mistake.

He parked the wagon in the churchyard and rushed Elizabeth into the building, knowing they were on the verge of being tardy. It was Daniel Parnell's turn to lead music, and he had just started a hymn as Luke hung his hat on a peg and stepped into the open sanctuary. Since all the pews were filled, he and Elizabeth stood at the back of the room with a few others.

When the congregation was seated, the Reverend Hill prayed and began his sermon. Partway into it, Luke scanned the room. The Coopers occupied their usual pew near the front, with Caleb and Cassy directly behind them. A woman was seated next to Cassy, then David and—

His gaze darted back to the woman. Jane. . .? A man shifted into his view, and Luke resituated himself to get another look. Her hair was the same deep shade of chocolate brown, but it was drawn up into a mass of curls on the top of her head, not scraped back into a tight knot. And she was not wearing gray or beige. Her dress was some curious mix between blue and purple, with tiny ruffles around the neckline.

But the woman had to be Jane. He would know her anywhere. Would know the graceful curve of her neck and her perfect posture. What was she doing here, when yesterday she wouldn't even leave her room? Thank the Lord he'd arrived late, and she hadn't seen him. He couldn't bear the hurt and blame he was bound to see on her face. He couldn't face her when he was too ashamed, too loaded down with guilt and remorse.

But he was supposed to have dinner at their house. How

could he sit across the table from her, loving her, when she despised him? He wouldn't go, that's all. He'd spare Jane from having to see him again. He'd have Elizabeth relay his regrets and go home.

&

Jane twirled the narrow ribbon around her finger, then unwound it, repeating the process unconsciously throughout the sermon. As hard as she tried to listen, her mind rebelliously strayed to the man she knew was sitting somewhere behind her. Knew it, because she could feel the hairs on the back of her neck standing on end.

What would she say to him? How could she apologize for her behavior? Undoubtedly, she would stutter and mumble. The words she'd spoken to him the day before replayed in her mind. No wonder he thought she blamed him for the accident. She'd not let him come near her and had ordered him from the room.

When the closing prayer came, she both welcomed and dreaded it. Knots of worry and apprehension curled in her stomach. How would she even manage to get him alone? She could not bear to suffer through an entire dinner without clearing the air first.

The pastor closed the prayer with a hardy "amen," and Jane rose to her feet with the congregation. Immediately, neighbors came by to greet her and extend their wishes for a speedy recovery. The ladies complimented her on her hair and gown but said nothing about the sutures streaking across her cheek. Ironically, she was unconcerned with her appearance, her thoughts instead on finding Luke.

When a lull came, she seized the opportunity to find him. Not seeing him, she walked casually to the back of the room and out the door, stopping only to greet the Reverend Hill. Luke wasn't among the small groups assembled on the lawn. Where could he have gone?

And then she saw him. He was riding away in his wagon, urging his horses to a brisk pace. Jane followed him with her eyes, her heart sinking as he passed the Coopers' place and kept right on going. He'd changed his mind and, undoubtedly, she was the reason.

Icy fear spread through her, freezing the smidgen of hope she'd had. Why, oh why, had she been so rude the day before? He didn't even want to see her, much less court her! Had he seen her face after all? Was that why he was avoiding her?

I am fearfully and wonderfully made. She repeated the words to herself until she felt at peace.

He'd attempted to see her many times, while she'd been feeling sorry for herself. It was her turn to make an effort. Even if he wanted her no longer, it was her responsibility to make things right with him and release him from his guilt.

Her family joined her then, and she followed silently as they walked the short distance to their home. She heard Elizabeth extend Luke's regrets and knew she'd been right about his sudden departure. He was avoiding her, and she couldn't blame him, after the way she'd behaved.

When they reached their house, she pulled her parents aside. "Papa, may I borrow one of your horses for a bit?" Her heart quivered with fear at the thought of riding again.

His brows winged upward. "Why, Jane, after your recent tumble from a horse, and you being such an inexperienced rider and all. . ."

"I can handle a horse now, Papa. Really. Don't worry about me."

Her father paused in surprise. "Well, what is it that can't wait until after dinner?"

Her mother surveyed her face, a small smile forming, then she nudged Eli in the ribs. "Stop being so nosy, husband." She winked at Jane. "Our daughter knows what she's about."

A short time later, she was seated on Satin and heading toward Luke's ranch. Within moments after mounting, her fear of riding was replaced with a fear of facing Luke. Her nerves twisted in a tight knot, choking her confidence. She might get her chance to talk privately with Luke, but what would he say? More importantly, what would *she* say? Would he believe her when she said she didn't blame him?

She nudged her mount to a slow trot. *All right, Jane. Just concentrate on your apology and your desire to relieve him of his guilt. That's your purpose in this little excursion. It is not about your feelings for him. It's not about winning him back.*

She gave a strangled laugh. Who was she kidding? Of course she hoped to win him back. She'd spent nearly two hours with Cassy this morning trying to make the most of her appearance just for today's confrontation. And she had never looked better—had never felt better about herself. She realized now, she had always felt unable to compete with her sisters, so she had inwardly chosen not to compete at all. Instead of making the most of what she'd had, she'd gone out of her way to hide it. Not that she was a beauty. No, she'd never be that. But she could accept the way God had made her and make the most of what she had.

When she turned into Luke's drive, her thoughts returned to the coming confrontation. *Concentrate on your apology. Concentrate on reassuring Luke.* She repeated the words to herself over and over, but somehow she couldn't convince her stubborn heart to smother the flicker of hope that burned there.

❧

Luke unharnessed the horses, his movements slowed by a weariness that belied his age. He'd gotten himself out of one pickle, only to find himself in another. He'd realized his feelings for Cassy were gone days ago and had confirmed his feelings when she and Caleb returned home yesterday. He'd known right away his feelings for Cassy had been shallow compared to how he felt about Jane.

And seeing the newlyweds' happiness had brought a mixture of joy and despair. Seeing their secret smiles and affectionate caresses had left him longing for his own matrimonial happiness. He could only imagine the joy of sharing his life with the woman who owned his heart. Why couldn't he have that?

Why couldn't he? What was stopping him, aside from his own fear? And when had he become such a coward that he was afraid of hearing the truth? Afraid of hearing the blame from his own beloved's mouth?

Luke halted, holding the horse's bit in his hands. Why was he running from his one hope of happiness? Jane may blame him, but if she did, he would hear her out like a man. Then he would tell her how he loved her and beg her forgiveness.

He put the bit back in Ranger's mouth. "Whoa, there, fella. Sorry to confuse you, but we've got someplace to go." Luke reharnessed the bays, working quickly with new purpose. He'd just started to climb aboard, when he heard the trod of an approaching horse's feet. Rounding the corner, he came up short.

Jane. He walked in a daze toward her, and she reined her horse to a halt. If he'd thought she'd looked different at church, the view from the front left him speechless. Curly tendrils framed her face, drawing attention to her almond-shaped brown eyes. Her chest heaved from exertion, and he noticed the delicate lacework in the bodice of her brightly colored gown.

Jane nodded her head tentatively. "Luke."

"Jane. What brings you out my way?" he asked, afraid to hope.

She toyed with the reins. "I. . .I came to apologize for my behavior yesterday."

His insides twisted. "You don't owe me an apology, Jane. I don't fault you for blaming me."

Her brows jolted upward. "But I don't! The accident wasn't your fault, Luke. Really, I don't blame you at all. We—Elizabeth and I—shouldn't have been sneaking up on you that way. You were hunting. Of course you would assume. . . Well, it was an accident, that's all."

Relief flowed through him at her ardent tone. Then he remembered the way she had rebuffed and rejected him the previous day. "If you don't blame me, why did you send me away? Why have you been avoiding me?"

Jane lowered her lids, ashamed of the way she'd felt and the way she'd treated him. "I guess I was simply feeling sorry for myself." She gave him a contrite grin as her gaze darted to his, then back down. "I've never been much to look at. Then, when the accident left me with this—" she covered the line of sutures on her face with her fingers, "—well, I just didn't think you'd ever be able to. . .to care for me."

Luke stepped closer, then reached up to cover the hand on her face. "Oh, Jane, you've always been beautiful in my eyes." The fervor in his eyes held her gaze. "When Cassy and Caleb returned, I knew right away what I'd suspected was true. My feelings for her were shallow. Nothing compares to the way I've come to feel about you."

Jane's breath caught in her lungs, her wary nature guarding her heart in case she'd misunderstood. She gathered her courage. "Does that—" She cleared her raspy throat. "Does that mean you still want to court me?"

Her heart quickened when Luke's mouth formed a smile, but when it turned into a full-bodied chuckle, she froze in place. Was he laughing at her?

Then she saw the familiar twinkle in his eyes. "Court you? Jane, I want to marry you." His expression grew serious, and she nearly drowned in those dark eyes. "That is, if you'll have me."

Her heart lurched. *He wants to marry me. Me. Plain Jane Cooper.* She couldn't have stopped the smile if she tried. "I'd be honored to be your wife, Luke Reiley."

Luke released a whoop of joy, then grabbed her around the waist, tenderly pulling her from the horse. She leaned toward him with her entire body.

All, that is, except her foot, which stuck in the stirrup. Before she knew what happened, she was flying toward the ground, a mass of limbs and petticoats. She landed with a thud on Luke, who released a puff of air on impact.

Quickly, she scrambled off beside him. "Are you all right?"

Luke met her gaze, stunned. His face broke into a smile when he realized that Jane had sustained no injuries. Then, his smile gave way to infectious laughter. "You know, that dismount still needs a little work!"

Her sense of humor took over, and she laughed along with him. "There's plenty of time for you to teach me."

His eyes shone with promise, holding her captive. "Yes, a lifetime."

A Letter To Our Readers

Dear Reader:

In order that we might better contribute to your reading enjoyment, we would appreciate your taking a few minutes to respond to the following questions. We welcome your comments and read each form and letter we receive. When completed, please return to the following:

Rebecca Germany, Fiction Editor
Heartsong Presents
PO Box 719
Uhrichsville, Ohio 44683

1. Did you enjoy reading *Never a Bride?*
   ❑ Very much. I would like to see more books
     by this author!
   ❑ Moderately
     I would have enjoyed it more if _____

     _____

     _____

2. Are you a member of **Heartsong Presents**? Yes ❑ No ❑
   If no, where did you purchase this book?_____

   _____

3. How would you rate, on a scale from 1 (poor) to 5 (superior),
   the cover design?_____

4. On a scale from 1 (poor) to 10 (superior), please rate the
   following elements.

   _____ Heroine   _____ Plot

   _____ Hero   _____ Inspirational theme

   _____ Setting   _____ Secondary characters

5. These characters were special because _____
_____
_____

6. How has this book inspired your life? _____
_____
_____

7. What settings would you like to see covered in future
   Heartsong Presents books? _____
_____
_____

8. What arc some inspirational themes you would like to see
   treated in future books? _____
_____
_____

9. Would you be interested in reading other **Heartsong
   Presents** titles?   Yes ☐   No ☐

10. Please check your age range:
    ☐ Under 18   ☐ 18-24   ☐ 25-34
    ☐ 35-45   ☐ 46-55   ☐ Over 55

11. How many hours per week do you read? _____

Name _____

Occupation _____

Address _____

City _____ State _____ Zip _____

Experience a family

saga that begins in 1860 when the painting of a homestead is first given to a young bride who leaves her beloved home of Laurelwood. Then follow the painting through a legacy of love that touches down in the years 1890, 1969, and finally today. Authors Sally Laity, Andrea Boeshaar, Yvonne Lehman, and DiAnn Mills have worked together to create a timeless treasure of four novellas in one collection.

paperback, 352 pages, 5 ³⁄₁₆" x 8"

❤ ❤ ❤ ❤ ❤ ❤ ❤ ❤ ❤ ❤ ❤ ❤ ❤ ❤ ❤ ❤ ❤

❤ ❤ ❤ ❤ ❤ ❤ ❤ ❤ ❤ ❤ ❤ ❤ ❤ ❤ ❤ ❤ ❤

····Hearts♥ng····

Any 12 *Heartsong Presents* titles for only $26.95 *

HISTORICAL ROMANCE IS CHEAPER BY THE DOZEN!
Buy any assortment of twelve *Heartsong Presents* titles and save 25% off of the already discounted price of $2.95 each!

*plus $1.00 shipping and handling per order and sales tax where applicable.

HEARTSONG PRESENTS TITLES AVAILABLE NOW:

(If ordering from this page, please remember to include it with the order form.)

......Presents......

Great Inspirational Romance at a Great Price!

Heartsong Presents books are inspirational romances in contemporary and historical settings, designed to give you an enjoyable, spirit-lifting reading experience. You can choose wonderfully written titles from some of today's best authors like Peggy Darty, Sally Laity, Tracie Peterson, Colleen L. Reece, Lauraine Snelling, and many others.

When ordering quantities less than twelve, above titles are $2.95 each.
Not all titles may be available at time of order.

Hearts♥ng Presents
Love Stories Are Rated G!

That's for godly, gratifying, and of course, great! If you love a thrilling love story, but don't appreciate the sordidness of some popular paperback romances, **Heartsong Presents** is for you. In fact, **Heartsong Presents** is the *only inspirational romance book club* featuring love stories where Christian faith is the primary ingredient in a marriage relationship.

Sign up today to receive your first set of four, never before published Christian romances. Send no money now; you will receive a bill with the first shipment. You may cancel at any time without obligation, and if you aren't completely satisfied with any selection, you may return the books for an immediate refund.

Imagine. . .four new romances every four weeks—two historical, two contemporary—with men and women like you who long to meet the one God has chosen as the love of their lives. . .all for the low price of $9.97 postpaid.

To join, simply complete the coupon below and mail to the address provided. **Heartsong Presents** romances are rated G for another reason: They'll arrive *Godspeed!*